Pride Publishing books by M.C. Roth

Single Books
The Drumbeat of His Heart
A Song for His Heart
Karma's Kiss

I0544787

KARMA'S KISS

M.C. ROTH

Karma's Kiss
ISBN # 978-1-83943-790-8
©Copyright M.C. Roth 2022
Cover Art by Kelly Martin ©Copyright April 2022
Interior text design by Claire Siemaszkiewicz
Pride Publishing

KARMA'S KISS

Dedication

For Q

Chapter One

"No. No. No," said Zack as he pushed the gas pedal all the way to the floor. The ancient car responded sluggishly, a full second passing before the engine vibrated with a purr that made his foot go numb. The bald tyres spun, trapped in a sheet of ice and snow that coated the road and the lone vehicle.

The storm sagged against the windshield as the wipers tried lethargically to keep up, leaving large, frosted streaks with every swipe. With each pass, the ice crystals grew denser, coating the wipers with budding globs of ice.

Another burst of wind battered the side of the car, fluttering against the door and buffeting the tiny cracks in the vehicle. A trickle of cold air brushed against his chilled knuckles, and a shiver cascaded though his body.

The vehicle lurched closer to the ditch that had disappeared into the blizzard's cloud. The tyres caught, edging sideways in a frozen rut. He jerked at the steering wheel, but there was no response as he was buried deeper in the drifts.

Zack's heart pounded as he lost control of the wheel and the engine sputtered. But he barely noticed as the car lurched into a stall or as the air got even colder through the flimsy heating vents. The storm was the furthest thing from his mind.

It had happened again. And, of course, it had chosen the moment when the biggest snowstorm of the decade was blowing its way across the lakes. The radar had probably gone from red to purple then black while he'd driven with no destination in mind.

The roads had been relatively clear a few hours before, when he had fled to his car, putting it straight into second gear before he even had his seat belt on. He had hit the highway, flipping a virtual coin to choose the exit he'd take before the heavy flakes had started drifting down from the grey sky.

He shuddered. His darkness — his curse — the thing had haunted him for as long as he could remember... It always seemed to choose the worst moments to rear its ugly, jealous head. This had to be one of the top five of all time, though.

He had tried to keep moving. He'd tried to leave before he could put anyone else at risk.

But he'd been sucked in by another pair of sweet blue eyes and a soft voice that had promised him a good night. That night had turned into a stream of great weeks and gentle touches that had him coming more consistently than he ever had.

The sex had been fantastic, if not a little bit soft, more often ending in his mouth or his hand — and not somewhere better, tighter and hotter. His nights hadn't been cold in an empty hotel bed or on a couch that he had claimed during a stranger's party. He had started to look forwards to waking up in the morning and seeing someone other than himself in his bed.

Then it had all gone wrong. One word and a spurned rejection, and his past had caught up with him with the force of a starving tiger. He'd staggered as he'd felt the blood drain from his face.

He had fled before anything could happen to the man who he had almost started to like. If he'd had the opportunity, he could have developed full-blown feelings, which were more dangerous than his curse.

He'd grabbed everything in sight that belonged to him, leaving more behind than he'd taken. His socks and underwear were lost beneath the bed and in the basket of laundry, but he hadn't had the time to retrieve them. They weren't the worst things that he'd ever left behind.

He'd had run to his ancient Honda, breathing hard by the time he had tugged the door open. As he'd sped away, he'd left another chunk of his past behind him, the sweet memories tainted by his bitter curse. The traffic had steadily thinned, until he was the only car in the midst of a forest that seconded as a snowy hell.

His trusty Honda was only five years younger than him and had more problems than he did, which was saying a lot. Its most recent issue was that it apparently couldn't drive through more than two centimetres of fresh snow.

He fumbled with the key, glancing out into the bleak stretch of swirling snow as he tried to start the engine yet again. Stomping on the gas, he waited for the RPMs to climb into the red zone before popping the clutch and putting the car directly into second gear. First gear didn't exactly work, and on ice, it was its own death trap.

There was a shuddering jerk that had relief flooding his gut, until the car rocked once and stalled back into silence. The dials dropped and the fuzzy radio station faded until the barest hint of the country song vanished under the sound of the wind.

"Shit," he said as he slammed his hand against the steering wheel. It shuddered, barely holding on to its rigging after his repeated abuse. He could imagine the wheel finally tumbling off as he merged lanes on a highway doing one-hundred-and-thirty-five kilometres per hour. *I'm lucky like that.*

His palm ached from the hit and the cold that was steadily seeping into the car, but it didn't stop him from slamming the wheel a second time. His thumb caught the edge of the horn, but the blaring sound was swept away on the wind.

The temperature inside the car noticeably dropped another few degrees, and his breath turned into a misty fog that coated everything it touched. The car's heater was lukewarm at best, and without a working defrost, ice had started to crust on even the inside of the windshield.

He turned the key again as he popped the car back into neutral and pushed the clutch to the floor. He shivered as another gust of wind cut into the Honda. His thin jacket was best suited for balmy fall days, but it was the only one that had been in sight as he'd scrambled to leave. His toes were numb in his sneakers, and his hands? Well, he was afraid to look at them, because he wouldn't be surprised if a few fingers were already missing. His gloves had been one of the many things that he had left behind, and his hands had been aching since the snow had started.

The car key turned under his hand, jingling with the other attached keys and mementos that he had picked up on his travels. There was a tiny metal sandal that he'd picked up in a beach town and an iron sun from a gift shop that he'd found in the middle of nowhere. The rest were worn, their edges smooth from their constant motion. He kept them close, so he wouldn't have to look back and remember.

The key turned, with the promise of escape and a hint of heat. *Silence*. Not even a putter from the flooded engine. His gut churned as a shiver racked his body. It was so freaking cold, and according to the last clear announcement on the radio, the storm was just getting started.

He grappled with the horn, pushing the button as hard as he could. There had to be someone close by who would come to his rescue if they heard him honking. People in the city might not have looked twice, but he was pretty far into the wilderness, on the only road that probably ever saw a plough in winter. People were different out here — lonelier.

The button clicked under his palm as the battery finally gave out. The same battery had lasted him twenty years, so, of course, it would choose to fail him when he was about to lose his toes.

Zack took a shuddering breath as his vision blurred and his heart sank. He wrapped his arms around himself, trying to keep the warmth from escaping. Perhaps everything was finally catching up with him. Freezing to death wouldn't be the worst way to go. He'd seen worse before — so much worse. His stomach clenched as memories fluttered to the surface of his mind. He tried to push them away before he could retch.

"Look at the snow. Just look at the snow," he said, holding himself tighter as he tried to focus on an individual flake in the whirling mass — anything to leave the flashes of his past behind.

Beyond the window he could see bits of the forest through the gaps in the gathering ice on the windshield. The road was nearly invisible, with no tyre tracks except his own behind him. Even those were almost gone now.

A green bough fluttered in the wind, dumping its heavy load onto the ground below it. A bird fluttered from the branch, battling against the wind as it took off. For a moment, it looked like it would lose the fight and be tossed into the nearest tree trunk. It pumped its wings faster, finally triumphing over the storm.

There were no hydro lines along the road or lamp posts that would guide a traveller along at night. It was a tourist's nightmare. He cursed himself, wondering if he should've taken the other fork in the road that had probably led along a path that was closer to the city.

A smudge of colour caught his eye as it flashed along the very edge of the trees. The trunks grew close together, dark and foreboding within the mass, and their limbs danced and swayed in the wind, dumping the snow back to the earth with each pass. There was so much movement that he wondered if he had imagined the blur.

He squinted and leaned closer to the window, trying to make sense of it through the fluttering snow. It could have been a deer. He'd already seen a few along the way, looking ready to jump out at his car and double his insurance. Or it could have been a bear, given how far he'd come, although he'd only ever seen them on television. The dark beacon had looked too small to be the creature he'd seen on *Planet Earth*.

He spotted it again as the wind stilled and the blizzard cleared for a moment. It moved through the snow with a fluid grace that could only belong to an animal who could survive a harsh winter. Nothing battered or beaten lived in this cold, and no predator could thrive without hunting in the perpetual storm that was February.

It grew closer with every loping step, until it seemed larger than what he imagined a bear would be. It was fast, too, cutting through the drifts as if it weighed nothing. Zack knew how hard it was to walk through snow that deep, which was why he usually avoided it at all costs. That, and he really didn't want to get his too-tight jeans wet.

Zack scrubbed the inside of the window with his nails, bits of ice stinging his numb fingertips. His breath frosted it over again, until everything blurred.

It could have been a dog with how dark the colouring was, but he'd never seen a dog that big. A bear would definitely make more sense, but according to the television, bears hibernated in the winter.

The ice on the window thickened into an opaque crystal as he pressed his forehead against it, desperate to see what was coming. It was running at a pace that was hardly possible over the covered ground, gliding over the snow without seeming to disturb it at all.

A bubble of fear simmered in his gut as he pictured a bear breaking through his window with its massive, clawed paws. He was small enough that he wouldn't be able to put up much of a fight, but there was still enough meat on him to make a decent meal, he supposed.

He took a deep breath, closing his eyes to try to ground himself. The wind around him paused, the car going suddenly still and silent. He snapped his eyes back open, looking through the tiny gaps from his fingertips. There was nothing but the dark tree trunks capped with pure white.

The seat creaked as he freed himself from the seatbelt and lifted himself to his knees, pressing against a strip of clear glass. He blinked, rubbing his eyes to remove the imagined fog, but nothing appeared. The snow was undisturbed, except for the partially covered ruts from his own tyres. There were no footprints, and no animal was out in the wind.

I'm officially losing my mind.

A loud knock sounded directly behind him, pushing a small scream through his lips. He slapped his hand over his mouth, muffling the noise as it battered his ears in the small space. He whirled around in his seat, his heart pounding as he spied something on the other side of the car. Whatever it was, it blocked the entire passenger-side window with its bulk.

The knock came again, a booming slam against the fragile window. It sent a shiver up his spine and straight to his core. How had anyone found him so fast? The road was deserted, and no one should have been able to hear the scream of his horn over the wind.

It could still be a bear. They were probably smart enough to knock. They could outsmart bees, for Christ's sake.

After a third knock, he stretched over the centre console to move closer, folding his legs up to his chest one by one so he could slide into the opposite seat. A muscle in his side twinged from the stretch, worse than any awkward position he'd been manhandled into.

The ice was thinner on this side, and he could see the outline of a dark shape but no details through the crystalised fog. It could have been anyone, or anything, but the knock was too loud and too annoying to ignore.

The handle was stiff as he pulled it, bracing against the wind as it surged again. The gust curled around door, ripping it from his grasp and flinging it wide with a crunch of metal. The shadow stepped back as the squall cut into the car with the strength of an iceberg, stealing the breath from his lips and sucking the remaining warmth from his limbs.

The shadow moved back into view, leaning down to peer at his prone body. It was nearly as wide as it was tall and took up the entire doorway, thankfully blocking the majority of the cruel wind.

Zack was able to get his first real look. It was completely covered in thick, dark fur, the strands clumped together with clinging snow and ice. He couldn't see a face, but his imagination created one for him, with snarling teeth that were whiter than the snow.

Zack's heart raced. It had to be a bear. *Why did I open the door for that?*

He took a deep breath, choking on the scent of wet fur, so similar to that of his childhood dog, Max, when he'd wandered out into the rain. It also brought him a strange sense of calm that he hadn't expected. It, at least, was familiar.

He gasped as gold eyes pinned him. They weren't yellow or jaundiced, but a glowing gold that almost seemed to resonate as they stared at him, unblinking.

He swallowed, his mouth dry and his throat clicking. It wasn't a bear at all—or even an animal. It was a man. He was covered in furs like some sort of reincarnated caveman, and his face was shadowed beneath a thick hood. His eyes were the only thing Zack could see through the gloom.

"Are you okay?" the stranger asked as he leaned into the car, blocking more of the wind with his bulk. His eyes weren't just gold, they were molten, drawing Zack in and stealing his breath. The scent of pine and woodsmoke clung to him, beneath the film of wet dog. His hands were wrapped in rough-looking leather that was cracked from either age or overuse, but the rest of him was hidden beneath the dark furs.

"I'm fine," said Zack, trying to keep his voice even. His heart was still thundering, but he could breathe again. An alarm was blaring in his head, and he suppressed the urge to reach for his keys. The car wouldn't start anyway.

He gripped his hands into fists to resist pushing the stranger away. He had to get out of there. He didn't want anyone else to get hurt.

A glint of white caught the light as the stranger pulled his lips back over his teeth and a low chuckle reverberated from his broad chest. "You don't look okay. This storm is going to last for a few days, and it'll take even longer than that to get the roads cleared. You shouldn't be out here in the first place. Are you an idiot, or are you just trying to get yourself killed?"

The gold eyes narrowed and Zack's heart beat so hard that his vision swam. The insult didn't matter to him, even though it made the hair stand on the back of his neck. It didn't matter to *him*, but it would matter to his curse.

The last time someone had called him an idiot, they'd ended up with two broken wrists. Zack had started running shortly after — once every offhand and cruel remark threatened the people close to him.

Zack tried to look past the man's bulk to the threats that could be looming from outside the car. The man could freeze in the storm, or a tree could collapse on top of him. It would seem like an accident...or a coincidence. It was always something that could happen to anyone who was unlucky enough.

He clenched his eyes shut and gripped the seat, waiting for the man to be maimed or injured. He knew it would happen quickly and without mercy. It always did.

He took one breath, then two, sinking deep into his core until he could hardly feel the cold. The shivering that racked his body ceased, and the ache drained from his fingers. Maybe his curse would take him this time, too, and put him out of his misery.

"Okay, now I know you aren't okay." The stranger's voice came again, so low and quiet against the rumble of the wind. Zack opened his eyes and met the glaring gold. He was watching Zack as if there were no storm around them at all — as if it were just the two of them in the world and they had nothing to fear.

Zack looked down at his trembling hands, the ache rushing back into them as he stared in disbelief.

The stranger was still alive. *How is he still here, looking at me like I have three heads?* He should be on the ground, twisted in some unimaginable way for the simple crime of calling Zack an idiot.

Zack reached for the stranger, tangling his fingers in the rough furs. They were stiff and coarse beneath his frozen nerves and so cold that it made him shudder. A clump of ice crumbled in his hand, and the pieces slipped down the sleeve of his jacket like tiny razor blades.

"How?" The word caught in Zack's throat as a sob tore from his chest. His vision blurred and his breath caught. *It isn't possible.*

"Here... Let me help you. I won't hurt you," said the stranger, speaking slowly as if Zack would try to run at any moment. His bulk blocked the rest of the wind, and the scent of pine, smoke and something else peaking as he leaned close. He wrapped his arms around Zack's waist and half-lifted, half-dragged him from the seat.

The fury of the storm beat at Zack's face, blinding him and bludgeoning his ears in a whirling roar. He tried to cry out as the needles of ice sharpened on his skin, but the sound was torn away. He could hardly breathe, even as his lungs begged for air.

He could never have imagined that winter could be like this. Winter for him meant sitting by a baseboard heater and looking through the window, complaining about the snow and the cold. It was about wearing so many layers that he looked like he had indulged in too many Tim Tam Slams, and it was about a perpetual howling wind that cut through the naked trees and narrow buildings.

This wasn't winter. It was an icy hell.

Zack's feet sank into the snow as the stranger tried to right him, and cold spilled over his old sneakers that had seen too many days. The tight green laces did nothing to protect him from the slithering crystals that slid up his pants and along his ankles, making his bones throb in protest. His feet were soaked in seconds.

The stranger's grip disappeared, and Zack fell against the Honda's unforgiving frame. It was the lightest shade of blue that would meld with the sky as he drove along on a fresh summer's day. Now, the same blue looked as frigid as his fingertips.

His face thudded against the roof as he lost his balance, his feet slipping on snow and ice as the taste of copper burst over his tongue, deep and rich, like sweet pennies. He thumped back into a drift, a spurt of fluff rising as he landed.

"Shit. Okay then," said the stranger as he hauled Zack back onto his feet before lifting him from the ground. He didn't even grunt or show any strain at all. He simply lifted him as if Zack weighed nothing, as if Zack were a child and not a man.

The man turned and started to walk, each step taking them farther from Zack's car and his only real safe haven. No matter what had gone down in the world, he'd always had his car to get away. Leaving it behind was like leaving his best friend, but he couldn't say anything, not when he was trembling so hard.

The man's feet glided over the snow, hardly sinking into the crunching powder and barely leaving a mark between the blowing drifts. His breath was silent, only a whisper of fog that filtered from his hood before it was swept away.

Zack had never been swept off his feet before, but now that the danger had seemed to pass, he was definitely on board. The stranger's body was hard and strong, his hands large and firm where they gripped under his legs and around his shoulders. Zack wasn't quite sure where to put *his* hands, or if he could even grip them, given how numb they felt, so he held them against his chest.

They moved down an unploughed road that had drifts that looked like they would be up to his waist.

There was barely enough room for a small car, and each side was blocked by impenetrable forest. The trees themselves were thick with curled bark that was wounded from age. It was no wonder that he hadn't even noticed the lane. It didn't look like it had been travelled for the entire winter.

Zack's eyelids sagged as his adrenalin finally started to fade, causing him to relax into the stranger's chest. There had to be something different about the man. He was the only person Zack had ever met who had been able to resist the power of his curse.

He snuggled into the warmth of the furs, shielding himself from the blowing snow that covered the man's footprints almost as fast as he could make them. Hopefully, he could still find the lane when it came time to leave. But right now, he just wanted to be warm again.

A tiny and haphazard-looking log cabin appeared out of the haze. It was a small and simple one-storey that had been carved out of logs stripped of their life and their bark. It was nothing like the beautiful identical logs that made up the cabins he'd seen before in magazines. This was rugged, like someone with no construction experience had attempted their first DIY and had managed to pull it off.

Smoke rose from the rough chimney, tossing the sweet smell of burning wood around the tiny clearing. It was the same scent that clung to the furs that were pressed against his cheek. The porch was unshovelled and heaped with snow, and the windows were dark and ominous.

It was unlike anything Zack had seen during his travels. He'd also never been half-kidnapped by someone in a snowstorm. Why couldn't it have been a billionaire who had happened upon him on the road? *Probably because they would have mobile data and weather reports, so they wouldn't be out in the first place.*

They crossed the threshold like a married couple, and Zack half-expected to be tossed on a bed and ravaged. He wouldn't have even minded at the moment. It would get him dry and so much warmer than he was now, and his standards weren't exactly high after looking for new places to stay for years. The stranger had beautiful eyes and was as strong as hell. Those were two out of the three boxes that Zack wanted checked for a good lay. Most days, he only required one.

A wave of heat engulfed him as the stranger stepped inside the cabin then closed the thick wooden door, locking a latch that rattled harshly in the wind. Prickling struck Zack's face first, before singeing his fingers and toes. The snow that had gathered on his hair melted and poured over his face to drip on the scraped wood floor beneath them.

The cabin was simple on the inside, too, almost shockingly so. Zack had lived in small places before, if rent prices had run too high to cover with the odd jobs he took to avoid touching his trust fund. But he had never had to subject himself to something this depressing. Even the nights that he'd slept in strangers' homes hadn't been quite so bad, because he knew that at some point he would be sleeping in a real bed again.

There was only one room—one perfectly square room that encased everything that someone needed to *survive*. The walls were stark wood logs that had something stuffed between them, keeping the wind and light at bay. The roaring fire flickered in an open hearth that had no barrier between itself and the rest of the room. It looked like the biggest fire hazard Zack had ever seen.

To the left of that, there was a kitchen that would have fit in a tiny home catalogue, with a single silver sink and a cupboard above and below it. Beyond that was a bed that was little more than a box spring and mattress on the floor, covered with a fur blanket that looked similar to what the stranger was wearing.

But beside the bed was the worst part of it all. There was a toilet and a small shower only feet from the front door and the bed. There were no walls separating them from the rest of the cabin—and certainly no door. The shower didn't even have a curtain. It was just an expanse of white over a tiled slab floor that had a drain in the centre. *And is that a watering can hanging from a hook at the top where a showerhead should be?*

"It'll be best if you take your clothes off before you sit in front of the fire. Everything is soaked from the storm, and there's still a chance of hypothermia if you sit around in something wet." The stranger made it sound like it was the most natural thing, to strip down naked in front of someone he didn't know. *This isn't a club or a frat party.*

Maybe it *was* natural for a man who was missing the 'room' in bathroom?

"I…" Zack paused, not sure what to say as he was lowered slowly to his feet. He dropped his hands he was using to hold on to the furs. He wasn't sure if he should thank the man, slap him or follow his directions.

"There should be some clothes by the bed that are clean. They won't fit you, but they'll be dry," said the stranger, cutting off Zack's whirling thoughts.

His feet were truly aching now and starting to throb in time with his heart. The idea of getting naked sounded better with every chunk of snow that melted and wicked into his jacket. It's not like he was bad off in the looks department, but he was very cold. He looked down at his groin. There wouldn't be much there to look at if the stranger watched him undress.

He looked around the cabin once more, searching for anyplace he could hide his dignity. Even a curtain would do, since there wasn't a door in sight except for the one that led outside. The windows were bare. There wasn't even a rod above them.

Who the hell is this guy? Even preppers have curtains.

He looked up from his internal debate as the door swung open again, snagging the heat from the room and chilling the water that had started to warm on his skin. The stranger took two steps out of the door, looking back over his shoulder with his eyes flashing in the blinding storm.

"I'll get your car off the road, so it doesn't get wrecked by the next plough."

The door slammed, and the storm retreated to the warmth of a crackling fire and the freezing dampness of his clothing. His shivering started again, and his teeth chattered so hard that he thought he might chip one.

He looked at the door, staring after the stranger and trying desperately to understand. Under the layers of sodden clothing and shivering skin, something bloomed in his chest that he hadn't dared feel since he had been a small boy with ambitions of taking on the world.

Hope.

Chapter Two

Zack glanced back at the door once, making sure that the rusted metal latch had caught so that the wind wouldn't push it right back open. There was no knob or anything coming close to a lock, just the latch. And it looked like it was made from scrap metal that had been left to rust in the rain for a few years.

He was truly soaked to the bone, but the air around him was so much warmer than the stormy outdoors. His toes ached as he freed them from his sneakers, the tips of them an alarming blue against the pink of the rest of his feet. He rubbed them softly, flinching at the sudden ache. The pain was probably a good sign.

He'd heard of people losing limbs to exposure in the distant past but not since the invention of indoor plumbing. He'd thought it wasn't something that could happen in the modern day — not when you could buy a pair of socks for twenty-six dollars that were rated for minus-forty degrees centigrade. He'd had some of those socks, as he'd loved the squishy soles, but they were gone now — probably lost under someone's bed.

His feet appeared promising, but his package was another issue. He peeled off his thin cotton boxers, revealing his shrunken bits. He was usually a good size when soft and just comfortably above average when he was hard, but now he was well on his way to an innie. Any longer in the snow, and his balls would have crept back into his body.

He sent a silent thank you towards the door, even more grateful that the stranger had retreated into the storm so he hadn't seen the dismal appearance of Zack's cock. There would be no second chance for *that* first impression.

There was nowhere to put the wet clothing, not even a laundry basket by the bed, so he stretched them out on the floor by the fire, hoping that they would dry on the flat surface. The wood snapped and crackled, sending tiny sparks into the air but dying out before they reached beyond the ring of red bricks that lined the hearth.

The wind howled and the fire twisted as air swept down to batter the flames. The smoke twirled, some of it escaping into the room before it was caught again and sucked up the chimney. Zack coughed as his eyes burned and the smoke blanketed him, soaking into his skin and hair.

He retreated from the flames, shivering as soon as he stepped away from the halo of light and warmth. It was dark in the cabin, with the only light sources being two windows and the roaring fire. Above, on the slightly peaked roof, there was nothing more than bare logs. There were no wires and no lines for water or anything else that he would consider essential.

The smell of something deep and rich hit his nose as he crept to the bed. It was the same scent that he had caught from the stranger that was mixed with smoke and pine, but now it was so much stronger, as if the bed had been soaked in it. It tickled his nose, stroking something deep in his mind. A shiver broke out on the surface of his skin.

The blanket over the bed was a thick brown fur that must have been from the same animal that the man had worn — or at least it's cousin. Zack wasn't sure what the animal had been, only that it would have had to have been huge for it to cover the entire bed — even though the bed looked like it was barely a double.

Beside the bed were two heaps of clothing. Some of them were furs, much like the one on the bed, only smaller and lighter, where others were actual clothing meant for real people. They were piled high, with no sign of order or organization.

He grasped the nearest sweater and brought it to his face, rubbing against the fabric in relief. It felt like the first thing from civilization that he had seen since he'd stepped off the edge of the earth and into the cabin. It even had legitimate logos from a familiar box store.

He smelled the cloth, looking between the two piles and trying to figure out if one was clean and the other dirty. The stranger had been right. There was no way that any of it would fit him. The man looked to be well over six feet, while Zack was a modest five-foot-nine and a half. They looked comfortable, though, and the fabric was soft under his fingertips.

Both piles had the same strong scent that engulfed the corner of the room. It was almost like a cologne, but unlike any he'd ever smelled while cruising through the men's section. It would have made his mouth water, too, if he hadn't been so cold.

He pulled the shirt he'd picked over his head, the rich green colour probably matching his eyes perfectly. It fell past his hips to settle beneath the curve of his ass, so it was long enough to hide anything from view if the stranger returned too soon—as long as he didn't bend over, at least.

There was a pair of jeans lower in the pile, but they were too wide for his thin hips and so long that he would have to roll them up enough times that they would cut off his circulation. He kept searching, finding a pair of loose fabric shorts with a drawstring near the bottom of the pile. He pulled them on and tugged the string tight so that the slick fabric wouldn't slip any farther down his hips.

He pushed the pile back to its place, heaping the clothes on top of each other again like stacking a mound of leaves. He shook his head. His room when he was a teenager hadn't been as bad as this mess.

There was a little space beside the bed that would fit a dresser perfectly. Zack nodded to himself, already planning the design of the dresser that he would buy as a thank-you gift. There were only a few good reasons for him to dip into his trust fund, and a thank-you gift was one of them.

Another shiver travelled up his spine, and he grasped the lone blanket from the bed before he wrapped it around himself and shuffled back to the fire. The fur blanket was heavier than it looked, but softer, too. The hair side was thick and coarse, but the opposite side had gone soft and silky, and it hugged his shoulders with surprising warmth.

The flames jumped and snapped as the wood burned down into bright coals that made his face ache as if he had a fresh sunburn. He couldn't remember the last time he'd sat at a fire, getting lost in the flames as they spun and writhed. It had probably been when he had been a child.

The floor was hard beneath his skinny ass, but there was no couch to sit on or any chairs at all in the tiny house. It was such a dismal place, and even the floor was rough, as if he could get a splinter at any moment. The stranger had taken minimalist and knocked it out of the virtual park.

The door opened again with a burst of cold air and a fluttering of flames. The cold only lasted a moment before the stranger stepped in and slammed the door behind him, cutting off the wind and clicking the latch shut once more. His furs were nearly white from the storm, but the heat of the fire soaked into them quickly, turning the crystals into a waterfall that dripped onto the naked floor.

Zack's mouth went dry as the man peeled off the fur that was draped over his shoulders. He'd thought the guy had been bulky and borderline obese from the way the furs hung on him. He was neither.

He was tall but also lean in a perfectly proportioned way that told of his strength. He was wearing a simple tank with cut-off sleeves and a pair of loose track pants that managed to cling to his broad, muscular thighs. His arms were like something out of Zack's dreams — the good dreams that left him hard and wanting. Their thick muscling wrapped up his wrists and corded around his biceps, triceps and up to his shoulders. His shirt was thin and tight enough that Zack could see two defined pecs and a stomach that was ribbed with more packs than he could count.

Zack wasn't bad off himself, and he could pick up a guy whenever he felt the need, but this guy was beyond. He was from another realm, where his body would be worshiped as a god.

Brown hair, flecked with an array of black, blond and red, fluttered down to the stranger's shoulders and framed his strong jaw that had a few days' worth of dark growth. The scruffiness would usually turn Zack off, but instead, he found himself cursing that he was getting hard in a thin pair of shorts that would hide nothing.

The stranger's gaze moved to Zack, and his nostrils flared as if he were seeing Zack for the first time. His gold eyes went wide as his chest heaved, sucking in heavy breaths through his nostrils.

Zack fought the urge to check his pits as the stranger stood there and *sniffed*. He couldn't remember if he'd put deodorant on before he'd scrambled out of his ex's apartment or not. There had just been too much on his mind.

"What are you wearing?" the stranger asked in a deep voice that was almost too low for the man's lithe body. Bundled up and looking larger than life, the voice had suited him, but now Zack wasn't so sure.

He didn't look away from Zack as he hung the soaking furs on a wooden hook next to the front door.

"You told me I could grab some of your clothes," said Zack, looking down at himself, suddenly unsure. Had he taken from the wrong pile? Wearing someone else's used shorts, when he hadn't found any evidence of underwear, was shudder-worthy.

The blanket covered most of Zack, leaving only his neck and the tips of his toes on display where it had come untucked. He realised that, in the right light, he could look naked beneath the cover.

"Don't worry, there is definitely something under this blanket. I hope these were okay to borrow?" He lowered the edge to show off a shoulder of green. Maybe the man was super attached to some of his clothes? But he hadn't said anything.

The stranger's eyes seemed to glow as he looked at the green weave on Zack's body. He was so much taller than Zack, and he definitely knew how to use every inch to his advantage.

The stranger took two steps, taking a loud breath through his nose as his eyes narrowed. "Who are you?" His voice was nearly a growl, and it made every hair on Zack's body stand up. The man sounded dangerous, and he looked practically lethal with his hands clenching into fists and the muscling on his arms flexing as he took another step.

"Zack," he said, shuffling up to his knees and dropping the blanket to the ground so he could make a quick escape. What were the odds he could find his way back to the road? Zero in shorts, and less if he had to run naked.

His heart fluttered in his chest, and his breath came in quick starts and stops with each step the stranger made. Zack stood to his full height, wishing he had an extra six inches on his frame so he didn't have to look up quite so far. There was no way he was going to win this fight. His idea of weightlifting was using a manual can opener…which was still too hard, in his opinion.

"What are you?" The stranger's deep voice rumbled, sending a shiver up Zack's body. Zack could feel the heat from the stranger, somehow even hotter than the fire at his side, and smell the smoky scent that was thick in the air.

"Zack," he repeated, not entirely sure what the man was asking. What kind of question was that? If he was asking sexual orientation, Zack was one hundred and ten percent gay, but that seemed a little personal before a proper introduction. They weren't in a bar, after all.

The stranger's lips twitched, curving up at the edges to reveal perfect white teeth that gleamed in the fire light. His nostrils flared again before he took a step back, turning his body away with his fists still clenched at his sides.

"Eric," said the stranger before he walked away, heading for the tiny kitchen that was only a few steps away. The fire snapped, making Zack flinch as the sparks arched towards his exposed legs.

It was probably the strangest introduction that Zack had ever encountered, and it had him rubbing the back of his neck and sitting on the rough floor. He scooted closer to the flames and rubbed his toes, glancing over to the man in the kitchen. Normal people would shake hands, but apparently in the bush, intimidation was the way to go.

He wasn't sure if the man, Eric, was rude or if he just hadn't talked to anyone in the last ten years. If the guy was just an asshole, it explained the cabin in the middle of nowhere, and it was probably a good thing. It was just too bad he looked like sex on legs.

"Okay then," Zack mumbled to himself and rubbed his hands together, the aching burn finally starting to fade. If the circumstances had been any better at all, he would have already been out of the door, trudging back to his car. His life was strange enough without this man hitching a ride on his baggage.

"Drink this," said Eric as a mug appeared in front of Zack's face and Zack started. He hadn't even heard the man approach, and the gesture seemed almost…nice. Unless the drink was poisoned…or roofied.

He grasped the mug, a glazed pottery piece that was blue and brown with swirling hints of orange. It was something that would never be able to go into a microwave or dishwasher, and the type of dish that Zack normally avoided at all costs.

He looked up and down the kitchen—not that the Eric even had a microwave…or electricity, it seemed.

He peered down into the mug at the murky liquid that smelled vaguely sweet. It was hard to see in the firelight as the sun rapidly drifted into night mode, leaving the windows blurry and dark. The firelight flickered, casting shadows everywhere in the tiny spaces. The demons of his darkness came out to play as the sun retreated behind the veil.

His mind dinged with alarm, screaming 'date rape' over and over as he sniffed the drink again. The smell was unfamiliar, another very bad sign, but the warmth of it was quickly spreading through the clay and into the palms of his hands. He was suddenly so thirsty that his mouth watered, longing for something to drink.

"What is it?" Zack asked quietly as he took a tentative sip, despite his best judgement. Unfortunately, his instincts tended to steer him in the wrong direction more often than not, so he was never quite sure when to listen to his gut.

"It's a dish of sweetened warm milk and spices," said Eric as he crouched down, tossing a log into the fire from the top of a pile that was haphazardly thrown next to the hearth. Bits of ash burst into the air, and dirt and bark rolled across the floor, unchecked. Zack had never realised that a wood fireplace could be such a messy thing. It had always seemed so romantic in theory.

"I had just warmed the milk when I heard your car horn, so it might be a bit cool." Eric stayed close to the flames as if there were no risk of his knuckle hair being singed. The fire swirled around the fresh wood, a wave of sparks flying into the air. Zack slid out of reach.

"It's interesting," said Zack, taking another small sip. It wasn't the worst thing he'd tasted before, but it was definitely foreign. His tastebuds didn't seem to know quite what to make of it, but it was warm in his throat and belly, at least. The third sip seemed a little bit better, and it was still hot, despite Eric's warning.

"Hmm-m, it would be better with fresh milk instead of powdered, but I make do." Eric tossed another log in the fire, sending a second wave of sparks into the room. Zack flinched, leaning out of the ring of heat. Fire safety wasn't his top skill, but he was pretty sure that you were supposed to set a log in a fire, not throw it in like a caveman would.

"But you wouldn't have needed it at all, if you weren't out in a storm like that," Eric continued, his voice light and losing its edge. "Running from something—or *someone*?" He turned and leaned on the fireplace mantel, his back against the heated brick that must've been cooler than Zack thought.

"How do you know that I'm not running *to* someone?" said Zack, unable to keep the bitterness out of his voice. He hadn't realised that he was so transparent. He set the cup on the ground with a clunk, empty of all but a few grains of sludge in the bottom. He never could bear to finish the dregs of anything, not even chocolate milk.

"No one is worth going through that," said Eric with a soft sigh as he shook his head and looked out of the window to where the storm was still raging. His lips were turned down, his forehead furrowed and his gold eyes glistening in the firelight. He sounded so...sad and so lonely that it broke a piece of Zack's mottled heart.

"Is that what you are doing out here alone in the woods? Running away?" asked Zack, cursing himself the moment he did. He wasn't normally a rude person, but Eric rubbed him the wrong way in every direction. He didn't want to be accused of running, even though that was exactly what he was doing. It made him sound like a coward.

Eric's eyes flashed as they caught the firelight, narrowing into piercing gold lines. He flexed his arms as he went rigid against the brick before he pushed himself off, turning away and stepping beyond the ring of firelight.

Zack's heart stilled as the milk curdled in his stomach. For a second, he'd thought that Eric might've actually been a nice guy. He had gone out of his way to help Zack, after all.

"I follow the hours of the sun, and I suggest you do the same until the storm passes," said Eric as he stepped towards the bed. He tugged at the hem of his shirt before he paused, smoothing the fabric down his belly and turning to Zack. "When the blizzard breaks, I'll take you back to your car and help you on your way."

"And if I want to go now?" asked Zack, his gut twisting into a tight ball as he imagined being trapped in this cabin for days with this beautiful man who was also one of the most confusing people he'd ever met.

"You are certainly welcome to try, but you'll end up with more than cold feet." He curled his lips over his white teeth, their gleam catching the firelight. This man was dangerous, and Zack had the sudden feeling that he wasn't going to survive to see the light of day, whether he stayed or not. He hoped his gut was wrong, as usual.

"Where do I sleep?" Zack asked quietly as the seriousness of the situation crept in. He couldn't camp out on the floor, but there was no other place except the bed — the tiny bed with a stranger who looked like he could strangle him with his pinkie finger.

"Use your imagination."

Chapter Three

Zack waited as long as he dared before he silently crept over to the bed, dragging the blanket behind him like a virgin's veil. His eyes were drooping and scratchy from staring at the fire for so long as he'd listened to the soft snores coming from the corner of the cabin.

He had looked back a few times to see Eric's shadowed face in the flickering light. Somehow, it became more beautiful with each glance. His long lashes fluttered in sleep, and his thin lips were parted, with just a hint of his tongue visible in the shadows.

Eric was even more attractive now that he wasn't prying into Zack's past or asking him questions about his orientation. Unfortunately, he topped the charts as one of the prettiest people who Zack had ever met.

Stretched out in sleep, the line of Eric's triceps flexed as he lifted his arm over his head, revealing fine, dark hairs that speckled his underarm. His hair was the most unusual colour that Zack had ever seen. If he were anyone else or someone who wasn't living in the middle of nowhere, then Zack would have sworn it was a fancy colour job. But out here, it screamed real to him.

He hovered over the bed for a full minute, glaring down at his sleeping companion that was hogging almost the entire bed. Most people would have done the polite thing when sharing — scooching to the side and turning towards the wall to leave space for a second person — but not Eric. He was sprawled across the mattress in a way that meant there was no way Zack wasn't getting at least partially mauled in his sleep.

He'd had worse before, and he'd slept with less attractive men for a night of escape and a warm bed that wasn't as lonely as a hotel room.

He turned away, shuffling to the toilet and looking back over his shoulder to make sure that he didn't have an audience before he freed himself from his borrowed shorts. The blanket sank to the floor, keeping his feet warm against the cold that seeped through the planks of wood. Away from the fire, it was so much colder, and the wind oozed through the tiny holes in the house. It was apparent that Eric had never heard of in-floor heating or insulation.

He reached for the handle on the scuffed toilet, but his hand slipped along chilled porcelain instead. He squinted in the low light as he searched for a glint of silver anywhere. Something glanced against his foot as he shimmied to the side while searching for the hidden handle — a foot pedal. It was like something from an outhouse at a local fair and not something that should have been in a house under any circumstances.

He shuddered, grabbing the blanket and shuffling back to the bed, only to stare down at the sleeping man again. The corner of Eric's shirt had ridden up, leaving a line of slightly tanned flesh naked to the cool air. There were no other blankets, except for the one that

Zack had stolen, but Eric didn't seem the least bit chilled.

That little glimpse of skin in the firelight made Zack's mouth water. He could see the groove of the v-line of Eric's groin, and the speckling of hair just above the track pants that hung low on his hips. The man didn't seem to be wearing anything underneath, and Zack couldn't recall seeing any boxers as he'd dug through the pile of clothing.

He wasn't sure if the lump he could see in Eric's pants was a trick of the shadows or a true outline. If it was real, then Zack was so ready to get jumped. The guy was an asshole, but he was fucking *hung*.

"Please stop staring at me and get into the bed." Eric's voice cut through the silence like a hot knife. His eyes were open, gold glowing, and watching as Zack stared at his package. His lips were a flat line, and he was obviously not a fan of the scrutiny.

Zack stumbled over an apology before he tossed the blanket onto the bed and followed quickly behind. "I just wanted to know what I'm getting myself into," he said, staying at the very edge of the bed as Eric remained where he was, sprawled in the middle. Eric was so close that Zack could feel his heat radiating across the small space and smell the woodsmoke on his skin. His gold eyes never looked away.

"And?" the stranger asked, rolling onto his side and shuffling back as his nostrils flared wide. He took a few deep breaths through his nose as Zack tried to get comfortable on the bed, shifting the blanket over his feet.

"Why do you keep smelling me?" asked Zack as he not-so-subtly sniffed at his armpit. He was a touch sweaty from going without a shower for the last two days, but nothing that someone should be able to smell across the room. He would have freshened his deodorant shortly before he got into bed, but the stick was probably frozen solid in the trunk of his car by now. He was not getting up to get it and he probably wouldn't be able to find his car in the dark, anyway.

The bed was comfier than he'd expected, with a pillow top and everything. He held himself taut at the edge, keeping his gaze fixed on Eric. The heat from Eric's body was quickly building up between them, and the smell of his sweat thickened. That strange scent was there, too, so much stronger with Eric so near.

He breathed deep through his own nose, trying to separate the scents in his mind. There was distant laundry detergent — thank God — and the ever-present smokiness from the fire. Beneath that was something that seemed to hover close to Eric's skin...something unique.

Zack pulled the blanket up so it covered his shoulders, keeping every bit of chilly air away from him. Eric's heat wrapped tighter, enfolding his body like a suffocating force. The man was like his own personal furnace. It was no wonder that he hadn't complained when Zack hadn't given up the blanket.

There was a sound of a deep breath before Eric huffed, shutting his eyes. "I'm just trying to figure something out, that's all." There was a rustle and the bed shifted as Eric moved.

Zack felt his cock twitch. Eric was beautiful, heavenly even, and it was only natural for Zack to want him. The heat radiating from him made Zack want to snuggle into his chest, despite the sweat that slicked his skin. He wanted to tuck his face against Eric's muscular neck and take a deep breath to see if he could start to piece together the puzzle in front of him.

He turned away, putting his back to Eric before the man could notice his steadily filling semi. Zack could feel the line of heat from his back to his hip, but he couldn't move any farther away without falling off the bed. He bit his lip, trying to stifle the building warmth in his groin.

"Can I?" Eric asked, his voice quiet, and tinged with the same desperate loneliness Zack had heard by the fire. He looked over his shoulder, willing the flush off his face.

There was only the space for a breath between them. Eric's hand was raised in the darkness, reaching his long fingers for Zack in the most personal way. Zack felt his face flush hotter as he nodded, numb from the lips down. He didn't know what the man was asking him, but if there was one thing Zack loved, it was to be touched. It didn't matter by who, or how, but to feel the connection of the press of someone else's naked skin was the greatest freedom in the world.

"Come here," said Eric as he slid his hand around Zack's waist and tugged him back into the middle of the bed. Zack let himself go, a gasp rushing through his lips as the warmth from Eric's arm soaked into his skin, making every hair on his body stand on end.

It was more than just a touch. It felt like something so much bigger, almost monumental, and it was like nothing he'd ever experienced before. Every nerve was firing, and his skin felt brand new, like freshly peeled sunburn. His cock was like steel from the simple touch.

Every hard line was solid against his back, and something else was nestling against his ass — something that was soft now but had the potential to be so much more. It already felt massive.

He shivered, sweat dripping down his back and wicking into his borrowed shirt.

The tip of a warm nose swept over Zack's neck as Eric took another deep breath, settling beneath his ear before a puff of warm air tickled his flesh. He trembled again as Eric pulled him tighter, engulfing him in warmth that was too blistering to be completely natural. He must've been suffering from hypothermia, after all, for Eric to feel that warm.

Something pinged in Zack's mind. The alarm was quickly muted as his cock flexed, and he let out a shocked gasp at the touch of skin against skin. It was as if there were a direct line from his neck to his cock. Eric's lips were so close to him — so close that he could turn his head to the side, and they would touch him. Zack wondered if they would be as soft as they looked.

"What are you?" Eric asked for the second time that day. His nose traced the line of Zack's jugular that was throbbing beneath his skin. His breath fluttered against Zack, so perfect and soft that it made Zack want to beg for more. He was touch-starved from holding himself back. He hadn't let someone hold him like this for as long as he could remember.

He had always pushed them away, too afraid what would happen if he got too close. But Eric had already proved that he was in no danger from Zack's curse. In fact, Zack could almost feel the darkness under his skin, purring at the contact and making him feel so alive that he wanted to scream with joy.

Zack was hard. His body didn't care if the guy behind him was out of his mind...or a dick. Even his better judgement didn't care at this point. There was an empty spot in his chest that had carved deeper every time he'd fled. Eric was searing into him, healing the wound as if it were never there in the first place.

He couldn't even imagine his ex's face right now, and for the life of him, he couldn't remember what colour his hair was. His mind was too overwhelmed with flashing gold eyes, and calico hair.

"I'm so gay," Zack breathed through dry lips. He flushed even hotter, his face feeling like he'd never left the fireside. He couldn't think straight, especially when Eric paused, and a huff of warm air burst over his skin as he laughed.

"Okay?" He didn't tighten his grip or let go, and the tickle of breath was fraying every nerve in Zack's body. Zack shifted on the bed, his ass accidentally pressing against Eric's groin.

Yes, accidentally, Zack tried to tell himself.

Something had grown, and it wasn't his imagination. It slipped between his cheeks like the best kind of invasion of privacy. Why hadn't he decided to sleep in the nude? He was definitely on board, and Eric seemed like he might be down with a little late-night action.

"Go to sleep," said Eric with his voice on the edge of a growl. He shifted his hips back and withdrew in a burst of chilly air. The bed groaned, and the blanket tugged on Zack's shoulders as Eric rolled away to face the frigid wall of the cabin.

There was a prickle of heat everywhere Eric had touched, and his groin was a throbbing mess. How could he ever expect to sleep now? His exhaustion had evaporated, leaving a buzzing horniness that would only recede with an orgasm.

"Wanna fuck?" Zack called into the darkness, slowly turning over to look at Eric's back. His tank top barely contained his flexing muscles. "I'm fully on board, if that's what was stopping you. I mean, you heroically rescued me from a storm, and you're hot as fuck. I'm down if you are." There was no question if the man was actually gay or not. No straight man would spoon another man and smell them for no particular reason.

He paused, waiting for an answer that never came. His cock caught against the heavy blanket as he rolled, making his toes curl. He fisted the furs, drawing his fingers through the tangled strands.

"I've been tested recently, too. I've been with other guys up until a few days ago, but I always used protection. Never done the bareback scene." Zack sat up and let the blanket fall to his waist. The air was cool, but he suddenly felt too hot for his own skin. He played with the hem of his shirt as he waited for an answer. There was a huff in the darkness, but the stranger didn't reply.

"You know, I usually don't have to beg for sex," said Zack, the first edge of anger seeping into his voice. He was so hard that it was starting to ache, and the scent of pine and smoke were doing nothing to quell it. If anything, it was making it worse, and he was barely holding back from plunging his hand in his pants and getting himself off. That seemed over the line, though.

"Did you consider that I'm just not that easy?" Eric replied, never twitching from his rigid pose. Even his voice sounded hot enough to melt snow, and it sent a whole new wave of sensation along Zack's spine. Christ, he wanted the man. He wasn't quite sure why, but he wanted him more than anything.

"I guess not." Zack let out a pinched sigh and took a few deep breaths, trying to clear his fuzzy head. The cloudiness didn't ease, and his cock throbbed painfully. "Do you care if I jerk off then, man? I don't think this is going away any time soon." To prove his point, his cock dribbled pre-cum on the inside of his borrowed shorts, the thought of gold eyes watching him making him that much hotter.

"Just…" Eric cut himself off and took another deep breath.

The blanket was thrown off the bed as Eric spun to face Zack. He gripped Zack's hips and tugged him back to the centre of the bed, laying Zack out beneath him.

The touch was strong enough to plant bruises deep in Zack's flesh, but the warmth soothed them at the same time, turning the ache into something so much better.

"You're still cold," said Eric as his eyes blazed in the darkness, reflecting every bit of firelight and more. He looked at Zack and the corner of his lips turned down.

Zack shivered. He felt warm — he really did — but there was an ache in his bones that just didn't feel right. It would also explain why Eric felt so much warmer them him, as if his body had been bathed in flames.

And now Eric, the beautiful man who had rescued him but had scarcely said a word, was pressing him into the mattress and looming in close. Zack arched up into the touch as Eric leaned in, his face nuzzling the crook of Zack's neck and his breath fluttering against his shivering skin.

Zack tried to grind up, but Eric stopped him, pushing his hips solidly into the bed. *Christ,* he was so strong. Zack didn't think he would be able to push Eric off, even if he tried — not that he was planning on trying anytime soon.

"You smell so good," said Eric, his voice a whisper against Zack's throat. The drag of wet lips over the column of his neck was enough to make Zack let out a shuddering breath. It felt so good, and Eric had hardly touched him. Each point of contact was like a brand on his skin, pulling pleasure from his very soul. He wanted so much more, but he wasn't sure how much he could take. He already felt like he was about to come, and the orgasm was bound to be strong enough to knock him into unconsciousness.

"Thank you?" Zack strained against the Eric, trying desperately to get some friction on his aching cock. No one had ever told him that he smelled good, and if they had, he probably would have taken two steps back and turned the other way. But sometimes beggars couldn't be choosers.

"I want to know what you taste like, but I don't know if I can hold back," Eric whispered over his pulse, mouthing softly but never tasting. He sounded like he was still fighting for control, though, despite Zack's writhing and moaning that would make a whore blush.

"You can fuck me hard. I like it hard." Zack gripped Eric's shoulders, trying to pull him closer, but he was shrugged off, thick corded muscle flexing under his hands. He tangled his fingers in the fitted sheet that stretched over the pillowtop.

"I'm not going to," Eric growled, flexing his hands painfully tight on Zack's hips. He bit his lower lip as he drew away and glowered at Zack, his every muscle taut.

"You have got to be fucking kidding me," Zack bucked up in the hold, but it was useless. Eric was just too strong. "Do something. Please." He never begged in bed...ever. It was too much of a risk if his partner said no. He didn't want his darkness rearing its head in the bedroom, of all places.

He usually just hitched along for the ride and went with the flow. The journey was half the fun, anyway.

This was different, though. He'd never wanted someone so badly before. He probably just needed to get it out of his system, so he could forget about Eric and the way his callused palms scraped against his skin. He had working hands, not the smooth, weak ones that some men had.

"Let me taste you."

"Please," Zack cried out as Eric's lips returned, this time pressing to his open ones. He'd been expecting Eric to lick his neck again, as that seemed to be some sort of kink for him. He didn't judge...not when he had a thing for ears himself. He loved perfect ears that he could suck into his mouth and lick as he fucked his partner — or they fucked him.

He hadn't been expecting those lips on his. The touch was so soft and open, their tongues touching before their lips had even become acquainted. Eric tasted the same way he smelled — hot, sweet and smoky with the scent of everlasting pine skimming over his tastebuds. He was slick and warm, and so fucking perfect that Zack couldn't stop himself from grabbing his hair and pulling him in deeper and harder.

Their tongues twined as they breathed in each other's air and tasted the slickness of their mouths. Zack groaned in the back of his throat, and he heard an answering noise, so much lower than his own. Eric removed his hands from his hips, and Zack surged upwards, bringing their bodies together as the kiss turned dirty. He throbbed in time with his heart, getting closer with every beat.

The air thickened between them as Eric threaded his hands into Zack's hair, tugging at the short blond strands that were just long enough to hold. The kiss hardened until Zack could scarcely breathe — and couldn't think to save his soul. It wasn't so much a kiss as his soul slowly being devoured by a man he hardly knew — a man he wanted so much that his gut ached with need.

Eric pulled back, and Zack whined high in his throat, begging without words.

Eric's chest was heaving, and his eyes were wide as he leaned back until he was settled on his heels between Zack's parted legs. Zack couldn't remember when he had slid between them. He could scarcely remember anything except the kiss.

His lips were still tingling as he swiped his tongue over them, needing every last drop of Eric. The man tasted so sweet, unlike the bitterness that he sometimes found when his partners used mouthwash.

Eric slid one hand to Zack's neck, and a drop of ice slithered down his spine. Gold eyes narrowed, and Eric curled his lips back in a snarl. He suddenly looked like a predator, ready to make a kill. He wasn't the same man as the one who'd brought Zack the strange warm milk.

"What are you?" Eric asked again as he tightened his grip on Zack's neck. The grasp trembled against Zack's skin, even as it tightened enough to make the blood start to roar through his temple.

Zack's hands flew up automatically, and he twined his fingers with Eric's, trying to tug him off. Eric's grip was solid, and somehow it sent the blood from Zack's brain much farther south, even as his heart pounded.

"I don't understand," Zack gasped, his hips rocking of their own accord. He was still hard, so painfully hard, and the more the hand tightened, the harder he became. He was in real danger, and his darkness should have appeared. It should have thrown itself at Eric and boiled him alive for calling him an idiot, but it hadn't. It was as if his curse had left him to his own devices at the worst moment.

The grip disappeared, and Eric leapt off the bed as if he'd been burned. His chest was still heaving, and his pupils were dilated in the low light, giving him the appearance of something wild and deranged. He clenched his hands into fists, as if he were trying to keep his hands off Zack, but Zack wasn't sure if Eric was keeping himself from fucking or killing him.

Eric turned away, his shoulders hunching as stepped towards the fire. Zack grasped the blanket, bringing it up and over his lap. The moment Eric pulled back, the thickness of his mind lifted, leaving only the chill of the night and the empty throb of his cock behind. He was so exposed on the bed, with his cock tenting his borrowed shorts and slipping through the mess inside them.

"Get some sleep," said Eric as he tossed a log into the fire, ignoring the sparks that splashed up at him. He walked to the door, pulling his furred coat on then jerking the door open. With a burst of wind, he disappeared into the dark swirling snow, slamming the door with the force of the gale and leaving Zack alone in the cabin.

Chapter Four

Zack rolled over in the too-soft bed, pulling the blanket closer. He blinked, his heavy eyes popping stubbornly back open. The uneven cracks in the door were just barely visible, and tiny bits of light had started to seep in as the night washed away into early pre-dawn. Sleep was no closer, even with the exhaustion that weighed heavily in his bones.

Eric hadn't returned to kill or consensually molest him through the night, and he wasn't sure if he was grateful or guilty. He was taking up Eric's bed, and he'd driven the man out into a lethal storm. The worst part was that he had finally found someone who seemed to be able to resist his curse, but he was alone…again.

The air had grown even colder after Eric's warmth had faded. The fire had sputtered low in the hearth, and although the blanket was surprisingly warm, it didn't keep his nose from getting chilled. The thought of pushing the blanket aside and going back out into the storm made him shiver. Even getting up to put more wood on the fire sounded painful.

He had no idea what had come over him, and he longed to apologise. He also needed to leave as soon as possible, hopefully *before* he humiliated himself even further. He couldn't believe that he'd thrown himself at Eric, like some kind of desperate slut. He honestly didn't know what had come over him.

Eric had sounded so angry, and for a real moment, Zack had thought that the night would be his last. Eric had been so strong, and it would have only taken one squeeze to finish Zack off.

He jumped as the door opened with a burst of wind and flurries as Eric returned, bringing a pile of firewood and a frigid chill with him. Eric stomped over to the hearth, tossing the sodden wood on the pile of logs, before he threw a few dry logs onto the blackened coals. Smoke swirled almost immediately, the bark curling and sparking.

He didn't even look over to Zack as he pulled the snow-encrusted coat from his shoulders to hang it on the hook. He returned to the smoking hearth, stirring the coals until they glowed red.

He still had on the same cut-off tank and track pants, but now the hem of the pants was dripping with ice. There were dark circles under his eyes, probably matching the ones on Zack's own face, and his face was drawn into taut misery. The deranged predatory look had retreated again, and Zack had no idea what he would be facing when Eric acknowledged him.

Zack's stomach had twisted into tiny knots the moment Eric had walked through the door. When he saw him looking so tired and forlorn, his guilt deepened until he felt more like floor scrapings than a decent human being.

"Sorry I came on to you," Zack finally managed to blurt out, his face flushing as he kept his gaze firmly fixed on the floor. "I really appreciated your help yesterday, and I think I just got a bit riled up. I'm sorry if I offended you."

His instinct was to try to defend himself. They had been in the same bed, after all, and his cock was barely controllable at the best of times. He held his tongue.

Zack heard the snort from across the room as Eric piled some thicker logs on the fire as it started to catch. Snow from one of them dripped down into the coals, sending a wave of sizzling steam in the air. The coals were still so hot, even after a night of neglect.

Eric hadn't looked his way yet, and Zack's guilt settled deeper. He really had pushed the line—with a stranger, no less. If Eric hadn't been so damn attractive, then none of it would have happened. Even now, the way his tanned shoulders shimmered in the firelight, made Zack want to put his mouth on them, so he could lick the salt from his skin.

Where is this coming from?

"If you help me back to my car, I can call a tow and be out of your hair. I don't think I'll be able to find my way on my own." He pushed the blanket past his thighs and shivered in the cold air. If his clothes were dry, he could be on his way before breakfast. He'd driven through worse before…not without snow tyres, but he would be fine.

"I can't do that," said Eric. He finally glanced at the bed, wiping his hands on his thighs before stalking to the kitchen. "If you go out there now, you'll die. This is the north, not the city. You don't have any choice but to stay until the storm has passed."

The windows glowed with early sunlight that must've been trapped behind a blanket of fluffy clouds. There were a few centimetres of snow plastered on the lower edge of the window that hadn't been there the night before. The storm was only supposed to get worse.

"Oh," said Zack, looking down at the blanket. "I could call someone?" He tilted his head, wondering who he would even contact. There was no one that he would put at risk, despite having their numbers programmed into his phone. The numbers were there so that one day he could reach them from a faraway place and ask for forgiveness.

"Don't go beating yourself up too much," said Eric, his gaze calling to Zack in a way that he couldn't refuse. "I left last night because I was afraid that I might lose control. I've never met someone quite like you, and I wasn't sure how to handle myself."

Eric looked away to pour water from a bucket on the wall into a thick black kettle. He strolled to the fire, using a poker stick to flip over one of the logs before he set the kettle into the midst of the coals. A splash of water spilled from its spout, turning red into inky black ash.

"I think I'll take that as a compliment," said Zack, the knot in his gut going slack. He looked down at his hands, but they looked just like anyone else's, even though there was a hidden power underneath. Eric couldn't possibly know about that.

"That you are unique?" asked Eric, crossing his arms and leaning against the brick. Shadows stretched over his face, and Zack's guilt prickled into existence again.

"No," said Zack, shaking his head. "That I'm so hot that you didn't think you could keep your hands to yourself. That's super flattering, man, and right back at you. But don't worry, my hands will be in my pockets for the rest of the storm, and I'll keep my thoughts about your abs to myself." It would be a difficult task — probably next to impossible — but he wouldn't go back on his word. He never did.

"You don't have to," said Eric as he stalked to the bed, bringing the warmth and smell of the fire with him. "Keep your hands to yourself, I mean. I've never had a kiss like that in my life." A blush bloomed across his cheeks, staining the tanned skin pale pink. He gnawed on his lower lip as he gazed down at Zack, his pupils wide in the low light.

"Me, either," said Zack, starting to lose himself. He couldn't have looked away, not even if someone had offered him a cure for his curse. He'd never seen a shade quite like it, like a hundred gold watches that had been melted down until they flowed so pure that they became priceless. "I have to know why you keep asking me what I am. What do you mean by that?" He continued to stare, waiting for the answer with terrified breath. *Does Eric know what I am?*

Eric hummed, breaking eye contact and turning to the fire. He grasped a metal hook beside the fire and lifted the kettle out of the flames, carrying it to the kitchen.

"You are unique," said Eric as he donned an oven mitt, pouring the steaming liquid into two cups. The scent of coffee filled the small space, bitter and thick, like the dregs at the bottom of a two-day-old cup.

Zack couldn't suppress a shudder at the thought of actually drinking instant coffee, which was the only thing in the world that smelled that bad. Coffee took one-and-a-half minutes to brew, and it was delicious. There was no sane reason to drink instant coffee.

He accepted the cup nonetheless as Eric handed it to him, holding the warm mug and letting the heat seep into his fingers through the clay. The black cloud swirled in the cup, sugar and cream free, and stinking like something that came out of the wrong end of a cat.

"Cream?" Zack asked hopefully before he remembered that he was in the middle of nowhere with no electricity. No electricity meant no fridge.

"I have powdered milk," said Eric as his lips curled into a smirk and he took a sip of his own coffee. He hummed in pleasure, taking a deep whiff of his cup before bringing it back to his lips. His throat bobbed as he swallowed it down, licking his lips and letting out another hum as he finished.

"Sugar, then? You *have* to have sugar. *Please* have sugar," said Zack, ready to fall to his knees and beg. Eric repeated the same action, dragging it out longer until Zack was ready to throttle him. *What an ass.*

There wasn't a type of sugar that Zack didn't like, and he would gladly welcome each and every one into his cup of bitter black. The smell was almost gag-worthy, but sugar might be able to save it.

"I don't, actually, but only because I ran out last week. I was going to head to the store yesterday, but then the storm rolled in." Eric shrugged and looked down at his empty cup. He turned to watch as the flames caught the fresh wood in the fire, the blacked ring of coals from the kettle receding to an ominous red glow. "I have cinnamon, though."

This day couldn't get much worse, and the sun was just barely peeking in the windows. Without coffee, there was only one way that he could function for the day, especially when he was already so exhausted. He didn't want to push the line again so soon, but Eric *had* said that it was okay.

"Can I kiss you?" asked Zack, setting his cup on the ground when he realised that he was never going to drink it. "You said you wouldn't mind, and since the coffee isn't edible, I have to find another way to wake myself up."

Eric's smirk died, and his brows rose in disbelief. Zack could almost hear the judgmental thoughts swirling through his beautiful head. He waited for Eric to make the first move, not wanting to crowd him and risk the same reaction as the night before.

"You never stop, do you?" It didn't sound like a question, just an observation. "Why do you want to kiss me so badly? And why are you trying to get into the pants of someone that you barely know?" Eric crossed his arms, a frown tugging at his lips as his eyes narrowed.

"Well, if that isn't the biggest question of my life, I don't know what is." Zack scuffed the floor with his naked foot, flinching as a sliver of wood threatened to pierce his skin. "I have trouble getting close to people, but when I see someone like you, someone who looks like they could blow my mind without even trying, I can never hold myself back."

"So, you jump in bed with a lot of guys then?" Eric's voice went hard, lowering into the same growl as the night before. The tiny hairs on Zack's arms stood up at the sound and he shook his head.

"No, I don't meet many people like you." It wasn't a complete lie. Zack had had a lot of guys, but he'd never met someone as infuriating and delicious as Eric.

Eric huffed. "I'll make a deal with you, Zack. If you pull your weight around here while you stay and prove that you are worth my time, then I'll give you your kiss."

"What does that mean?"

Eric laughed, a sound that shook his body and reverberated in the cabin.

Why do I always have to open my big mouth?

* * * *

A list. An actual fucking list of chores, as if he were a twelve-year-old trying to earn an allowance. Eric handed it to him with a laugh when Zack eagerly agreed to *pull his weight*, so ready to prove that he wasn't a perverted leech.

Some of the things on it, his own mother never would have asked him to do. Most likely because they'd had three housekeepers, and Zack had never touched a washing machine while he had been living at home…but that wasn't the point.

Is a kiss really worth it? With any other guy he'd met in his life, the answer would have been no. But Eric was different. Eric didn't look at him the same way that other men did.

Which was exactly why he found himself melting a bucket of snow in front of the fire to fill up the toilet's small water tank. He hadn't even known that plumbing like that was an actual thing until Eric had pulled the lid off to show him. As far as he had known, toilets flushed, and if there was an outhouse in the park that didn't, he avoided it unless the situation was dire.

The snow was still blowing when he bundled up in his dry jacket and pushed his way into the storm. He shivered as the cold quickly overwhelmed the heat of the cabin, sinking into the top layer of his skin, as if his jacket were a layer of cellophane.

He carried his empty bucket like a lost child looking for a well, sinking into the drift that had consumed the front steps. Eric's footsteps had faded to tiny divots in the drift, even though he hadn't been gone long at all.

Zack cast his gaze out into the storm, cringing as snow seeped through his lashes and assaulted his eyes. Fuck, it stung. Why was winter so...wintery? How far would he have to go to fill the bucket? Eric hadn't given him any details, other than *"Fill the bucket. Use snow."*

He rolled his eyes at himself as he looked down to his legs. His knees were just visible above the devirginized snow, but everything below that was hidden and freezing. One scoop, and the bucket was brimming.

About to turn back to the cabin, a glint of colour caught his eyes. It was no wonder that he hadn't noticed it before, because it was nearly buried beneath a two-metre-high drift. His car beckoned to him, along with his bag of clothes and his cell that were both within.

He had no idea how his vehicle had even got to the cabin with all the snow and the tiny lane, but he shrugged it off. Eric had been gone all night, after all, and would have had more than enough time to get the car back here, even shovelling by hand. He certainly had the muscles for it.

He was able to grab his bag and his phone out of it before his hands started to ache. He ducked back into the cabin, tapping at the blank screen of his phone. It didn't respond.

He gratefully applied a frozen strip of deodorant, revelling in his lack of body odour as he pulled on a fresh, cold T-shirt and pair of jeans. He wasn't cold for long as he waited for his bucket of snow to melt before dumping it into the tank. Water splashed down the sides of the toilet and all over the floor, soaking his pants and his freshly donned socks.

Grabbing a towel, he scrubbed the floor dry, cringing as the cloth came away nearly black. The shower didn't look much better off, now that he was eye-level with it, and the rest of the floor was dusty at best.

If there was one thing that he had learned while he was away from three housekeepers, it was that he couldn't stand a messy house. He was convinced that half the guys he'd met kept him around simply because he cleaned their places. And yet, his socks had always managed to go missing.

Then there were a few dishes in the sink and the pile of ashes in the never-ending fire. Warming up the kettle had been an experience that he hoped not to repeat. Eric had made it look so easy, but Zack burnt himself three times and singed the hair off one of his knuckles, and the water was still only warmish when he poured it into the sink.

He had almost burned the place down taking the ashes out, but besides that, Zack was almost grateful for the number of chores. There was no television or internet, but he hadn't had a moment to be bored.

Eric had returned for a few brief snacks that consisted of an unidentifiable jerky that Zack was determined never to eat again. He hadn't removed his furs or even looked around the cabin before he turned back out into the storm.

The jerky kept Zack's hunger at bay as he downed another glass of water, leaning against the wall as he wiped the sweat from his forehead. Everything from his face to his pits were starting to feel very gross, and the sweat dripping down his back was not helping. He was attempting to mop, but he wasn't sure that it was actually possible. The water was just smearing around on his make-shift mop, that consisted of a ratty dark towel he'd found at the bottom of one of the piles.

He tried the phone again, only to find it dead and silent. The battery was probably fried from sitting out in the cold for so long, and he doubted that Eric would be much help with it. He had hardly seen the man all day, anyway, except when he'd stuck his head inside the door to grab a snack.

A growl rose from his stomach at the same time something scratched at the thick wooden door. He glanced over his shoulder and lifted himself to his feet as the scratch came again. It sounded like a dog, but his sweepings had been dog-hair free. Maybe Eric was one of those guys who had the 'pets stay outdoors because they totally understand traffic safety' attitudes. The poor thing was probably freezing.

Zack pulled the door latch up, sliding it free from its metal housing and cracking the entrance to look outside. The cold air soaked directly into the damp spots on his pants. He crinkled his nose. Jeans were the worst when they got wet, but they made his ass look so much better.

He only had a moment to look outside before a sudden gust of wind pummelled him, sending him stumbling back. The cold dried the sweat on his skin instantly and put every hair on high alert. The fire fluttered in the hearth as the wind struck it with full force.

He blinked slowly as he caught sight of what was standing in the narrow cabin door that had flung wide. Snow started to creep over the rough threshold, some of it melting instantly as it met the warmer air that was steadily escaping.

Standing amongst the gathering drift was some kind of dog, but it was bigger than any dog he could ever remember seeing. It had a long, sandy-coloured coat that was streaked with mud and bits of copper near its muzzle. Its shiny black lips were pulled back over its sharp, white teeth as it snarled, its yellow eyes glaring at him.

His heart pounded. *It's a fucking wolf.*

"What the fuck," said Zack as he stumbled back, tripping over his own feet and landing hard on his ass, sending an ache all the way up his spine. His stomach twisted as the wolf advanced, its snarl deepening to a dark growl as it took two steps into the cabin. The footprints it left in the snow were massive, like the ones a Great Dane might make.

It paused, one foot raised as turned its snout up, scenting the air. Its long pink tongue licked its snout as it sneezed once, its sickly gaze never leaving Zack's prone form. Eyes like that were what nightmares were made of.

Zack shivered and tried to push back, but his feet slipped uselessly against the floor. The wood had been rough, almost threatening splinters before he went at it with a broom and polish. Death by DIY lemon Pledge.

The wolf advanced, its head cocked as it licked its lips, its tongue dragging over the speckle of copper that Zack finally recognised as blood. Its tail wagged, slow and ominous, but its eyes never changed from their soulless pits. Snow was tangled in its coat and large clumps stuck to its paws, jiggling with each forward's step before melting onto the wood.

Zack took a deep breath and held it as the wolf stepped over him, sticking its nose directly in his face and huffing again, a soft growl rumbling through its throat. One paw struck his stomach, pushing him back to the ground as sharp claws dug into the soft skin of his belly. Its leg was heavy and so strong that he knew he didn't stand a chance.

This is how I'm going to die. His curse had finally caught up to him and had decided that it was his turn. *No more hurting anybody, and no more running.* He thought he would've felt relief to finally be free, but instead, stone-cold fear settled into his chest and made it impossible to breathe.

He squeezed his eyes shut as teeth settled over the column of his throat, pressing on the delicate skin hard enough to bruise. Fangs burned hot against his skin, as if coals from the fire had landed there, melting through his defences. He could feel the animal's breath on his flesh and smell the taint of every exhale as it brushed over his face. His stomach clenched and threatened to spill.

The wolf pushed its paw harder as it flexed its teeth, sending blood rushing to his head as they seared hotter. He could smell rancid meat and the deep scent that always accompanied canines. His heart pounded in his chest as another growl shook from its throat, sending vibrations directly into his skin.

"Stop!"

Zack heard the yell but couldn't bring himself to open his eyes. It was probably his imagination. There was no way that he could be saved twice within twenty-four hours.

But it sounded like Eric, his voice was deeper than he'd ever heard it.

There was a yelp, then the weight of the paw and the press of teeth left him. A second yelp followed a thump that sounded loud enough to break bones. The stale smell of dog drifted away, but his neck still burned where the saliva was quickly drying on his skin.

He pried his eyes open, terrified of what he was going to see. In the movies, there was always a bigger animal or a bigger fish in the pond. Something that could rip a wolf off him and throw it hard enough to make the wooden beams of the house tremble had to be massive and strong. Teeth at his throat and dog breath would be the least of his worries.

Eric stood just inside the cabin, his hood tossed down and snow tangling in his hair as it raged in the wind. His eyes shone like liquid gold pouring into a mould, and his hands were clenched hard enough that veins popped up along his knuckles. He was growling, so much deeper than he ever had, and the hairs stood up on the back of Zack's neck.

The wolf was across the room, piled at the base of the wall like a heap of furs, but he was rising fast. His yellow eyes never left Zack, even as he shook his head to throw off the blow that Eric had dealt.

"You don't touch him," said Eric, striding to the wolf and gripping him by the back of the neck to scruff him. The wolf struggled and snarled, gnashing his teeth before he turned and sank them into Eric's arm. Blood poured from the wound as Eric let out a yelp, his hands going slack.

The wolf lunged at Zack, where he still lay frozen to the floor, watching the display even as more snow drifted inside the door. Those teeth had cut through Eric's skin like nothing, and now they were coming back for him. He would die before he even had the chance to contract rabies from the sick animal. It had to be sick. Every nature program he'd ever watched had said that wolves never attacked humans unless they were starving, and this one didn't look the least bit hungry.

Eric threw himself after the wolf, knocking the beast to the side as it tried to jump over Zack again. With a grunt and a canine whimper, Eric settled over Zack, his hips lining up between Zack's spread legs and his arms on either side of Zack's head. He was all strength, with every muscle pulled taut, visible even with the furs around his shoulders.

His weight hit Zack, then the warmth of Eric sank in. Every memory from the night before rushed in — the weight of Eric's hands on his hips, and the rise of his cock against Zack's ass. Even with danger across the room, Zack was already gone. His mind was a foggy mess, and something buzzed under his skin — something that had always been there but was stronger now than ever before.

The moment that the outline of Eric's soft cock lined up with Zack's, Zack cut back a moan. He wasn't sure if it was because of fear or adrenalin, but he was hard in an instant, throbbing and dripping a bead of pre-cum that smeared on the inside of his boxers. He could taste the metallic bite of Eric's blood in the air, layered over the heat of Eric, and his mouth watered, craving more than just the promised kiss.

"He's mine," Eric growled, glowering at the wolf. His words were barely discernible over the roar of blood in Zack's ears, but the sheer possession in the tone made his stomach clench with desire. He'd never belonged to anyone, but the way those words sounded on Eric's lips had him yearning for just that.

The wolf somehow seemed to understand Eric, as he snarled and circled around them. His tail was upright and pointed over his back, still waving aggressively as he lunged and skirted back every few steps.

"I'm sorry," said Eric, finally looking to Zack for the first time. His golden eyes pierced into Zack, and he was filled with everything that was Eric. His body relaxed of its own accord, his head falling back to the floor, even as he rutted up into Eric's cock. He could feel the man stirring against him, going impossibly hard as his pupils dilated.

Eric leaned back a scant inch, pulling the draping furs from his shoulders and tossing them in a damp pile by the door before he settled his weight back down on Zack. A wave of warmth engulfed Zack that was nearly overwhelming, as the layers slimmed down to almost nothing. He could see the outline of Eric's pecs through his thin tank top, his nipples peaked from the cold.

He wanted to run his fingers over the solid nubs and lean down to suck one into his mouth, swirling his tongue around it and letting the tiny hairs tickle his tongue. The danger of the wolf took a distant second place to his overwhelming thoughts of tasting and fucking the man on top of him.

Zack gasped as Eric shifted between his legs, pressing their lengths together near-painfully. Then Eric's smooth lips were pressing against his own, stealing the smothered breath from his lungs. Eric's mouth was already open, his tongue seeking and twining with Zack's in the most overwhelming way.

The man tasted like heat and fire, with a distant twang from the jerky they'd snacked on earlier. Eric moved like he was wild and untamed, and his lips tore Zack apart, one slick slide at a time. Eric brought his hand to Zack's throat before he slid back around to cup the base of his skull, pulling him up to meet every touch.

Zack fisted Eric's shirt, trying to somehow pull the man closer. The dejected whine and the retreating click of paws meant nothing to him, especially when he swallowed their combined flavours that were accumulating in his mouth. He would have to make a point to always be underneath Eric, so he could do that over and over. He wanted everything that Eric had to offer.

"Sorry… He can be a bit off with strangers," said Eric, his voice strained and low, and he ground down into Zack. He leaned back in, sucking Zack's tongue into his mouth, and momentarily making his mind go blank.

"You have a fucking wolf. A little warning would be great next time," Zack replied, trying, and failing to pull Eric back for another kiss. His cock was so hard that he was almost there. Just a few more grinds, and he would come.

"He's not a wolf." Eric chuckled and shook his head before he leaned back on his knees. Zack could see the outline of Eric's cock against his thin jeans. It looked so fucking thick that it probably had its own devoted cult following. His mouth watered at the thought of tasting it.

"I know what dogs look like, and that was *not* a dog." Zack licked his lips and dropped his hands as Eric lifted off him and subtly adjusted himself. Eric snorted, raising one dark eyebrow.

"He's a coyote, not a wolf. Trust me, if it was a wolf, you would have shat yourself for real. He's been around for years and sometimes he just follows me home. He must've smelled you and come to investigate."

Zack sat up and took another whiff of his armpits. His frozen deodorant had done an okay job, but definitely wasn't five-star. "Sorry... My deodorant froze in the storm, and I think that killed it a bit." He palmed his cock through his pants, still ready to be thrown in bed. Eric turned away and closed the door, cutting off the frigid wind. He hardly looked affected except for the bulge in his pants.

"It's getting late, Zackary. We should eat and turn in for the night." The light beyond the windows was getting dimmer, even though it was hard to tell through the continually blowing flurries.

"Do I still get my kiss?" asked Zack, grinding his teeth to keep from cursing Eric. If there was a football team named 'mixed messages', Eric was the MVP.

Eric looked around the cabin, from the freshly washed sink to the almost-dry water stains all over the floor. He blinked once, lifting his brows.

"I actually didn't expect you to do anything on that list, to be honest." He looked over to the fire at the near ash-free base. Zack had left the red-hot coals, skimming along the cloudy border instead. It wasn't perfect, but it was a hell of a lot better than it had been.

"I might be a city kid, but I know how to work — especially when I'm bored out of my mind," said Zack.

He didn't mention that his idea of hard work was going to the basement to reboot the router or locating his cell-phone charger after being drunk.

"Then please allow me to feed you, then thank you properly for a job well done." Eric eyed a water puddle a second time and the dripping towel hanging from the hook where his coat would normally sit. "Or a job done, at least."

Zack licked his lips, searching for any remaining taste. "I'm looking forward to it."

Chapter Five

"Eric?" Zack asked once his dick had calmed down enough that he could follow the man into the kitchen without the risk of groping his ass. The floor squeaked under his foot where a nail must've been loose on the thick boards.

Now that the floors were cleaner, he could see the little worn pathways in the places that Eric usually walked, and the rougher bits around the edges of the cabin. Zack followed one path, eyeing the natural grain that he had become very accustomed to. Compared to laminate it was ugly and bland, but the natural look was starting to grow on him — along with their owner — even if he had left Zack aching and hard more than once.

"Yes?" asked Eric, looking back with a soft smile. "And I need you to move." He looked so innocent, as if he hadn't just laid Zack out on the floor. His pants had smoothed out, and he no longer had the biggest erection that Zack had almost seen.

Zack shifted, the floor squeaking a second time as he looked down at his feet. He was honestly surprised that he'd only managed to get one sliver while he'd been scrubbing on his hands and knees. Luckily, there'd been an ancient pair of tweezers in the small cupboard near the toilet. He could sense a tetanus shot in his future.

Eric shooed Zack to the side, so he was standing well away from the squeaky bit of flooring. Eric crouched, feeling along the seam of the wood until something came free in his hands. Zack stumbled back as Eric lifted the wood so it squealed open on hinges that remained hidden. A dark stairway appeared out of nowhere, dipping out of sight.

Zack's heart thudded fast. The wolf *had* been the least of his problems. He was about to get tossed into a sex dungeon, never to be seen again. His cock twitched for unknown reasons, even as he backed away another step. He was far enough from civilisation that no one would hear him scream.

His panic must've shown on his face because Eric quirked an eyebrow, subtly scenting the air. It was something that he did constantly when he was in Zack's presence, almost like a nervous tic.

"It's just a root cellar and cold storage. Did you want to see?" Eric asked as he dropped down a few feet through the hole to the first step. He crouched so his bulk fit in the small space, before he started down the steps, disappearing into the darkness.

"Nope," said Zack, his heart still pounding. It was like every horror movie he'd ever seen. *Lost in the woods with no escape. A quiet man, who converses with wolves, has a hidden basement below the floorboards.* His mind whirled.

Maybe Eric was off the grid because he was hiding from someone or something. But if he truly meant to hurt Zack, then his curse would stop him...*right?* His darkness had always kept him from harm, even as a child. It was only as he grew older that it gripped him tighter in possessive claws.

Eric reappeared with something that looked like meat wrapped in thick pink paper in his hands. There was a cobweb sticking to his hair just above his eye, leaving a trail of dust down the side of his face.

"Here," said Eric as he passed the slab of meat to Zack. It was way colder than a freezer should ever be, with crystals marring the outside of a package. He peeled back the crinkling paper to find a raw roast that made his stomach grumble. A few spices and a decent oven and he could have it tasting fabulous. But of course, there was no oven, and who knew what kind of spices Eric had when he didn't even have sugar.

"Beef?" Zack asked as he turned it over in his hands, his fingers going numb from the cold. Something about it looked a little bit off, and the edges were ragged, not like the clean cuts he would find in a grocery store.

"Venison." Eric lifted himself out of the hole, his arms bulging in a way that was very distracting. Zack swallowed as he blatantly stared, wondering when they would get to the kissing part.

"You should have a shower while I get this thawed out and cooking," said Eric as he lowered the wooden floor seamlessly back into place. Other than the squeak, no one would ever know it was there.

"You're telling me I stink?" Zack asked, breaking out into a smile before he remembered the shower setup. There was no curtain, no door and no shower head. Just a watering can on a hook. He still hadn't figured out how that was supposed to work, but as he took a whiff of himself, he realised that it was definitely necessary.

"Your scent is...distracting," said Eric after a long pause. He pulled the meat from Zack's hands and set it on the tiny countertop. When he turned back to Zack, he towered over him.

Zack let out a shudder as Eric ducked down and nosed at his neck. His head fell back, leaving himself open for the man to take whatever he wanted. He was ready to beg to be taken down to the sex dungeon in hopes that he could relieve some of the heat that was snapping between them.

"Every time I come back in here, I smell you and I almost lose control." Eric's lips moved over Zack's throat as he spoke, and Zack let out a high groan. "When I saw him on top of you, trying to claim what's mine, I almost took you right there. Fuck, I wanted to." He scraped his teeth over the bruises left behind by the wolf — coyote — whatever.

"Why did you stop? I already told you that I want you," said Zack, his voice nothing more than a trembling whisper. He wanted Eric's lips and teeth all over his body, teasing him in whichever way he wanted to. Then he wanted to return the favour and suck the man hard enough to make him see stars.

"You aren't ready for me, honey. And no matter how much you want me and I want you, we just weren't made for each other. I don't want to hurt you," said Eric.

He gripped Eric's shoulders as the man whispered against his neck, dragging his fingers down to brace against Eric's hips. He trailed over the peak of Eric's groin, unable to hold himself back any longer. Eric hadn't said no, and maybe he was just as nervous as Zack with the unknown spark between them.

"Jesus," said Zack as he moved his hand around to cup the tent in Eric's pants. He was so hard and so thick that he would be nearly impossible to take. He was long, too. The mere outline made him shudder. It twitched violently as he strummed his finger over the tip. Whether the man was cut or not, it would still be sensitive.

"We could try," said Zack, groaning as possessive teeth nibbled his flesh then nipped hard as he squeezed the shaft in his hands. "I mean, if a guy on the internet can take a fist, then I should be able to take you. Determination is key." He felt his rim clench as he said it. Eric would literally ruin him for any other man, but for some reason, he was okay with that.

"There are things you don't know about me that would be difficult for you to understand," said Eric as he pulled back and licked his lips. His pupils were blown wide, like a wolf on a full moon.

"Are you a serial killer?" asked Zack, going tense despite himself as he thought of the hidden basement.

The hands on his hips dropped away, and Eric turned, roaring with laughter. It was a loud, throaty laugh that brought a blush to his face instantly and a smile to Zack's lips.

It was the first time Zack had heard him laugh, and he was determined to hear that sound as many times as possible.

"No," said Eric, shaking his head and wiping the tears from his eyes. "Just shower and I'll make dinner." He shook his head as if he could remove Zack's presence. It stung with how easy he made it look. Zack was still reeling, his heart caught in his throat and his cock throbbing. He couldn't wait for his promised kiss.

"How do I shower?" said Zack, his heart still fluttering at the memory of that beautiful laughter. He looked to the hook and the watering can, completely stumped. He wasn't a garden, after all.

"Typically, it starts with you taking your clothes off. Then you get wet, lather and shampoo, then rinse. Repeat if necessary." Eric's lips were still curled in a dazzling smile, but his sarcasm put an edge to the words.

"I'm not an idiot," said Zack as the first bubble of frustration appeared in his gut. People had been calling him that all his life. He was too innocent, too afraid and too clueless…an idiot. Most of those people were gone now.

"You have no water," said Zack, failing to keep all the bite from his voice.

"I was just teasing," said Eric, looking like he wasn't going to stop teasing Zack any time soon. "Pipes would freeze out here in the winter, so I have to make do with a watering can. It's just like the water for the sink when you did the dishes. Boil some in the kettle, then mix it with cold from the barrel. I usually take the bucket over, too, to refill the can halfway."

"Oh," said Zack, biting back an apology of his own. It wasn't his fault that he could be sensitive at times. "And what am I supposed to do about the curtain?" asked Zack, looking at the shower that was so exposed on the other side of the room. He wanted this man, yes, but he wasn't sure if he wanted his first naked experience to be a voyeuristic one. And he was still hard, too.

"You'll have to trust me not to look, and I'll have to trust you to do the same when I take my turn next."

Zack stumbled on nothing, his feet nearly going out from under him. There was no question as to if he would watch Eric shower. He absolutely would. There was nothing short of a restraining order that would stop him. And he was basically getting permission if he could catch Eric watching him.

He lifted his shirt over his head and tossed it to the floor, already scrambling for the button on his pants. His fingers tripped over themselves, snagging on the fabric and the button.

"Wait!" Eric called, slapping one hand over his face to cover his eyes. "At least give me the chance to turn around. And you still have to heat the water." A blush creeped down his neck, disappearing below his tank top.

"Oh, come on. I'm not that bad." Zack let out a sigh and gave up on his button, heading for the kettle and the pail, filling both and depositing the kettle into the flames. He hissed as the heat singed the hair on his arms, stripping it from his knuckles and turning it to ash. "I'm not a supermodel or anything, but I've got a nice body."

"That's not what I meant," said Eric, peeking through his fingers and dropping his hand when he saw that the coast was clear. "I want to preserve your virtue, not steal it away just for a look."

Now it was Zack's turn to laugh, the noise muffled by an oven mitt that he held in his teeth. "My virtue?" He spat out the cloth that tasted of stale grease and spices. "Buddy, that ship sailed a long time ago. That is sweet of you, though, to believe I'm so virtuous."

The kettle whistled, and he gripped it with the mitt, pouring it into the bucket then swirling the water around with his hands until it was just on the side of too hot. He grabbed the watering can, repeating the same process. At least it was a nice watering can, and not one of the rusted metal ones that would be forgot in the garden until there were more holes than flowers.

"Is that why you keep pushing me away? Because you're afraid I'll steal *your* virtue?" Zack asked, still chuckling. He paused, his hand freezing in the lukewarm watering can. Eric hadn't answered. He was dangerously quiet.

"Shit, are you a virgin?" Zack felt his eyes go wide as he looked up and down the blushing giant. "How is that even possible?" The man had the body of a god and his kisses had melted Zack's panties.

"I'm not," said Eric in a voice that was not at all convincing. "I've just never been with someone—someone like you." His golden eyes were downcast, looking back to the kitchen and the forgotten roast.

"A man?" Zack's heart clenched. He'd always wanted to steal someone's anal virginity, but it just hadn't been in the cards before. The men he slept with were experienced and good at what they did.

"No, I've been with men before." Eric stuttered, his gaze dropping to the floor as if the wood were suddenly the most interesting thing in the world. "Just not someone so different than me...so fragile."

Fragile. He'd never been called that, not in his entire life. And he hated it.

"You might think you're the big bad wolf, buddy, but I've seen worse and had bigger." Zack snorted as Eric's blush deepened. "But if it makes you happy, please avert thine eyes to spare dost fragile virtue."

"You might be surprised," said Eric, turning to the meat. His back was an impenetrable wall that cut Zack off in a way that left him unbalanced.

He shook his head. This man was an enigma, and sometimes an asshole, but he was also intriguing...and hot as fuck.

Zack carried the rest of the water over to the shower, only pulling one muscle along the way when he twisted too far. Rubbing his side, he stripped his pants, willing his semi into dormancy as he stepped onto the tile then the white fiberglass floor of the shower. The surface was frigid beneath his toes, and he could almost feel the wind soaking through the shower wall. Screw the pipes freezing... He would freeze, too, if he didn't get this over with soon.

He grabbed the soap and shampoo on offer, sniffing them and nodding in approval. The soap was normal, with very little scent at all, but the shampoo was pine. It wasn't as strong as Eric, who smelled like he had just rubbed one out with a Christmas tree, but strong enough that it filled his nose and cleared the lingering dark thoughts from his mind.

Twice this man had insulted him, and twice he'd lived through it with nothing more than a stubborn blush. Maybe Eric did have something to hide, but then, so did Zack.

He hung the watering can up on the hook that jutted out from the shower wall. He could tell it was an after-installation addition from the jagged holes in the fiberglass and the peeling red paint on the hook. But it worked better than he'd thought it would.

Hot water that was probably just a touch too hot on his cooled skin poured from the can in a steady stream of tiny raindrops that soaked his short hair and body efficiently.

He peeked out into the cabin a few times as he showered — once just after he'd rinsed the shampoo from his hair and again as he soaped his cock and ran his hands over his sac and back to his entrance. He was tight and puckered, not used to anything more than casual hook-ups with average dicks, in every sense of the word. He could only imagine how far his pucker would have to stretch to accommodate the dick across the room — or if it even could.

Eric set a grate over the flames as soap dribbled between Zack's thighs in white, scented streaks. He circled his entrance with one finger, imagining how Eric would touch him while he watched the man set the meat on the rack, it sizzling as it touched the metal. He sank inside with the tip of his middle finger, the soap slick but irritating against his rim. A tiny groan worked its way from his throat.

Gold eyes flickered his way.

It was only a flash, but it was all Zack needed. He now officially had permission to watch Eric in the shower. *Thank God*. If he made Eric touch himself now, would that give him the green light to jerk off to the show? Before he could decide, the water ran empty, and he was left shivering.

Drying and putting his clothes back on was a much speedier affair. He finished in front of the fire, taking a whiff of the cooking meat and running his hands through his short hair to comb the strands. He'd taken advantage of Eric's shaving razor earlier, but his face was already starting to feel scruffy again.

"So now that you know I'm a natural blond, it's your turn," said Zack, a leering smile splitting his face.

"I didn't mean to," said Eric as he looked away and stroked the fire with a heavy brass poker. "I just thought I heard something, and I wanted to make sure you were okay."

"My hero," Zack sang, flopping down by the fire and leaning back on his hands. "I hope I smell better, anyway." He shrugged and watched the dancing flames, letting them take him away. They were beautiful, each flame an individual, like a unique snowflake.

He jumped when he felt something on his neck. He hadn't even heard Eric move behind him, but there he was, his nose shivering over Zack's skin as he took a deep breath.

"You smell like me now—and like you." Warm lips nibbled on him, and Zack let out a groan. He reached for Eric, but the man dodged him easily, always just out of reach.

"I want you," said Zack, giving up all pretence and putting his heart out on top of the grate, along with the roast.

"I know. I can smell it," said Eric as he took another deep breath against Zack's shoulder. "When I found you, you smelled of the city with a hint of citrus and something else dark, so dark that I could not begin to fathom it. Now there are trees there—and coyotes and me. The darkness can't fight all that."

Zack froze. *His darkness? What does Eric know?*

He was starting to think that he'd lost his curse somewhere out in the snow. But Eric was saying that it had been here all along. It wasn't possible... Eric wouldn't be crouching there if his darkness was still with him.

"Are you a chef?" asked Zack, his mind still whirling at the possibilities as he attempted to change the subject. Eric had struck too close to home. "I've heard you have to have a great sense of smell to be a chef and that the good ones can tell how old a wine is just by its flavour." Nothing else made sense—nothing that wasn't beyond the realm of possibility, at least.

"No," said Eric, moving his teeth to the back of Zack's neck and pressing down. "Your guesses are getting colder."

"Closer to a serial killer than a chef. Should I be concerned?" asked Zack, looking over his shoulder as Eric pulled back, a veil shuttering over his eyes.

"Yes."

Chapter Six

Despite his promises to himself, Zack managed, barely, to keep his eyes from the corner of the room as Eric showered and changed. He'd almost looked when he thought he heard a gasp, but instead he kept his eyes trained on the wooden floor. He suddenly had no desire to visually molest this man without his explicit consent, no matter what his dick had to say about it.

His mind was whirling as the cooking venison filled the room with rich smells and the sounds of sizzling fat. The storm swirled against the windows, snow creeping halfway up the panes, but the cabin was warm. The pile of firewood had grown throughout the day, and the flames roared gratefully.

Closer to a serial killer than a chef... So Eric wasn't a cannibal. Maybe he was just a killer, hold the 'serial'. But something about that didn't fit. Eric had been nothing but helpful with a side of asshole.

Things were starting to add up, like a checklist from social media that revealed his movie character personality.

Cabin in the woods…check.
Giant wolf-like coyote obeyed him…check.
Talking about claiming Zack…check.
Sniffing Zack constantly and calling him his…check.

Holy shit. He'd seen this survey before, although he'd laughed when it had claimed he was a gremlin. *Eric is a bloody werewolf.*

Zack's heart pounded as Eric padded past him with bare feet and a sleeveless tank. He was in shorts, even though the fire was only hot enough to keep the cabin at a balmy seventeen centigrade.

"Looks like it's getting there." Eric reached into the flames, poking the roasting venison with his pointer finger before he drew back, sucking the juice from his fingertip.

Immunity to cold and hot temperatures…check.

The man was so strong and was lined with lean muscles that covered every part of his body that Zack had seen. His body temperature seemed high, too, probably to keep his faster metabolism going at an epic speed. He'd read that in a book once.

Zack took a few deep breaths, trying to calm himself. Eric hadn't hurt him or even threatened to hurt him, despite his self-proclaimed struggles for control. His worst assault was continuing to call Zack an idiot.

He obviously had enough strength that he could kill Zack without a second thought, but Zack had an ace up his sleeve, too. He was probably more dangerous than Eric, even if the guy was a fucking werewolf.

"When I was twelve, I baked cookies for one of my neighbours," said Zack, catching Eric's attention and tensing further as his gold gaze snapped to him. Why hadn't he questioned their colour? No one had eyes like that.

Gold eyes like a wolf…check.

"She turned her nose up at the cookies, as if I were insulting her by not offering her something that was gluten, sugar, soy, lactose and peanut-free." Zack shook his head, trying to keep his emotions in check. It had been a long time ago, but it still pissed him off. A shiver crept under his skin, and his arms prickled. Eric's nostrils flared, his pupils dilating. "I was so upset, so I vowed that I would never talk to her or bring her cookies again. The next day, I found out that she had fallen shortly after and had broken both of her wrists. She couldn't cook herself anything with those casts on, but I never took anything over after that."

"Okay?" asked Eric, his eyes narrowing with concern. Never taking his eyes off Zack, he ran his fingers through his hair as he leaned towards the flames. Steam rose from his hair as he got too close. He was fearless.

"A couple of years later, I got my first job and had my first crush. He was just so beautiful that I couldn't help myself. I had to kiss him. My boss saw us and fired me. He said it was because I couldn't date a fellow employee, but I think it was because he couldn't stand having a gay kid working for him. I stormed out, but I heard that a few minutes later he fell down the stairs. He couldn't work, and he ended up losing his job, his house and his kids before the end of the year. I don't know where he is now." It had felt so good at first, when his crush had told him about what had happened. But as he'd watched the man's life fall apart, the warmth had faded into inexplicable guilt.

"Then there was my first *real* boyfriend, Josh. I was sixteen and I thought I was ready to go all the way, even when I wasn't. He pushed me when I said no, and he burned to death in a fire that night." Zack swallowed loudly, his throat clicking as his mouth went dry. The fire had started shortly after he'd left the building in tears, his body aching and bruised, and his spirit momentarily crushed. He remembered cursing Josh and wishing that he was dead. Minutes later…he was.

"So you're unlucky?" asked Eric, obviously still trying to catch on. He dropped his hands from his hair and let it hang in soggy clumps around his face. Bits of it were already drying, fluffing up in a rainbow of colours.

Zack let out a humourless laugh and glared into the flames. Thinking about his teenage years was worse than nails on a chalk board. And saying it aloud made him want to puke.

"That's what I thought, too, until it got worse. My next boyfriend cheated on me, and he died in a car crash that afternoon. The one after that slipped on ice and ended up in a vegetative state when he told me he wanted to break up. The next one told me he got a chick pregnant, and he got impaled by an icicle when he walked out of the door. It fell off the roof and went right through his skull. That's when I started running."

"I don't understand," said Eric, shifting so his long body was stretched out on the floor in front of the fire. His arms glistened in the firelight, and his skin was still damp from the shower. "None of those things were your fault."

"Yes, they were," Zack hissed, slapping his hands against the wooden floor with a bang that thudded through the cabin. "Every single one of them was. If someone said no to me, they ended up hurt. If they pushed me away, they ended up dead. The darkness you said you could smell on me, it's real, and it has haunted me my entire life." He blinked, but he was unable to keep the tears from falling.

"But I insulted you, told you no and pushed you away. Nothing has happened to me," said Eric as he sat up and shuffled closer, the heat of him searing through Zack. Zack turned to him, curling his face into Eric's strong chest before letting himself breathe deep. Pine and smoke and something dark.

"I think it's because you're like me. You aren't the same, but you have your own darkness." Zack looked up through watery eyes to the beautiful man who held him. His gold eyes were wide, his chest rising rapidly. "You're a werewolf, aren't you?" said Zack, both expecting and dreading a howl of agreement to burst from Eric's throat. Maybe Eric would throw him out the door and give him back to his wolf friend to finish what he started.

What he didn't expect was a laugh—a deep, dark chuckle that sent a bolt of terror into his very soul. It wasn't the loose, joyful sound from before. This was the laugh of a predator, chuckling at his prey's demise.

"No, Zack, I'm not a werewolf," Eric growled, his lips curling back into a snarl. "I'm so much worse."

Chapter Seven

"O-oh, I'm sorry. I just assumed," Zack stuttered, trying and failing to pull himself away from Eric's chest. Eric had gripped him in a savage hug, his fingers digging bruises into Zack's back.

The werewolves in his imagination were giant beasts that stood seven feet tall with over three hundred pounds of muscle strapped to their elongated frames. They had huge yellow teeth dripping with saliva, and red eyes that rolled back in their head when they bit you. What could be worse than that?

"You just have all the hallmark traits of a werewolf, so I just thought...do werewolves exist?" He wasn't sure why he was asking questions when he should have been struggling to get away. Eric wasn't furry right now, but that could change in a heartbeat.

"Yes," said Eric, still clutching Zack and refusing to let him budge. He sniffed the top of Zack's head, burying himself in his blond locks.

Zack's feeble struggles ceased as a thrill went all the way down his spine, and his world opened wide before him. He wasn't the only freak out there, struggling to find someone or something to connect with. There were others out there, too, and it sounded like some of them were worse off than himself. He might have been cursed, but at least he didn't howl at the moon...or whatever else werewolves did.

"But you aren't one?" Zack asked, looking into Eric's gold eyes and losing himself for a moment. What could be worse than a werewolf? He racked his brain for other creatures he had imagined late at night in a lonely bed. How many times had he pictured something out of his imagination between his thighs or on top of him? Too many to count, not that he would ever admit it. They were fantasies for a reason.

"I'm not one," replied Eric, his voice smooth as he swallowed a growl. His eyes were bright and predatory— like he could consume Zack at any moment.

"Hotter or colder?" Zack asked, swallowing hard and licking his dry lips. Eric's grip had loosened, but he refused to be the one to pull away, not when it felt so good to be in Eric's arms. "Am I hotter or colder? Are you closer to a serial killer or a werewolf?" He needed somewhere to start his round of twenty questions.

He pulled Eric closer when he felt the man shift like he was trying to stand. He wasn't ready to let go yet. Eric was the only one he had met that was somewhat like him. It didn't matter that he was a bit of a dick or that he had turned Zack down more times than he cared to count.

"The meat will burn," said Eric, pulling back, even as Zack tightened his hold on his shirt.

"Stop avoiding the question. The meat will be fine," said Zack, taking the opportunity to skim his fingers over the shoulders beneath his grasp. Eric was built, and he could have tossed Zack off him if he really wanted to.

"Hotter, I imagine," Eric replied, extracting himself and flipping the venison roast on the rack...with his bare hands. He'd at least used tongs before, but now that the pretence of normalcy had faded, he must've not felt the need to pretend any longer.

"I know you aren't a vampire. Vampires are terrified of fire," said Zack, settling back on his ass and moving his feet closer to the flames. He wanted to curl back into Eric's lap, but he obviously wasn't wanted there.

"You seem so sure of yourself," said Eric, his confident smirk back on his face, and his voice biting with sarcasm. He licked his fingers clean, his teeth catching the firelight.

"Well, I guess you do like my neck. You actually seem a little obsessed with it, now that I think about it. And you did nibble on me." Zack hummed, tapping his finger against his chin.

"I'm not a vampire," Eric snarled, letting out a huff as a blush spread over the bridge of his nose. He dropped his gaze to the floor.

Well...that was new. This version of Eric was downright bashful, and it was so much easier to overlook that he was also a prick.

"Thank goodness," said Zack with a sigh." Don't get me wrong... I love a good vampire story, but I always wondered about iron deficiency for the ones they bite. Do they take prenatal vitamins? How do they get all those vitamins back that the vampires are eating? And biting during sex? I'm not sure I want something razor sharp inside my neck when I'm getting fucked to the edge of my life."

"You are the strangest person I've ever met in my life, and I'm a lot older than I look," said Eric as he pushed off the floor and made his way to the kitchen. He returned with a sharp knife and two plates before slicing off two hunks of roast, letting the juices dribble down off his fingers and into the fire where they sizzled and spit. He placed a piece on each plate before he sucked his fingers into his mouth, swirling his tongue around each digit.

Zack watched, too distracted by the sight of Eric's tongue wrapped around his fingers to wonder how old he really was. He looked like a man in his late twenties, maybe early thirties, but that was... *Oh God.*

Eric sucked hard, pulling off with a pop that was close to pornographic. *Definitely not a virgin, then.* Zack could imagine him doing the same thing to his cock, sucking at the head and licking down his shaft with that pink tongue.

When he caught Zack's gaze, he lifted one brow as if he had no idea what he was doing. His flush had vanished, and his smirk fluttered back across his lips.

"Are you going to tell me what you are, or do I have to keep guessing?" asked Zack, shaking his head and reaching for the steaming piece of venison. His stomach grumbled with a steady low growl as the scent engulfed him, like beef, with a little something extra. He gasped and dropped it back to his plate. "Holy fuck, that's hot." He shook his hand, then sucked his fingers into his mouth, but it was too late. His fingertips felt like he'd dipped them into molten lava.

"I'm enjoying your guesses." Eric let out a small smile and bit into his piece, tearing it off. His teeth didn't look any larger than average and certainly not any sharper, but he tore through the chunk like it was edible paper.

Zack felt along his own teeth, trying to compare them to what he saw before him. His were dull from too many days chewing on gum to avoid grinding them. He still had them all, even with his colossal sweet tooth.

Zack blew on his fingers, and the meat, waiting for the sharp tingle to pass before he reached for it again. When it *finally* hit his mouth, he couldn't stop his face from twisting.

It wasn't so much the taste, which was definitely gamey, but the texture was… interesting. His jaw would be stronger by the end of the meal, and he would have a new appreciation for marinade.

"Do you know what I am?" asked Zack quietly. He didn't think he was the same thing as Eric, but he never considered he could be more than just a walking bad-luck charm.

"No, I don't." Eric polished off what was on his plate before cutting off a second steaming piece, shoving the entire thing into his mouth and chewing loudly.

Zack took another small bite, letting out a soft sigh as he chewed and chewed. He was right about the spices. The meat needed about six hours of marinating and three dozen spices before it would actually be acceptable to eat. It did, at least, calm his aching stomach, but he was already dreading the inbound heartburn.

Zack finished his piece but couldn't bring himself to reach for a second. He'd had enough, barely, but his jaw was aching, and his stomach was fluttering for a different reason. Watching someone eat had never been erotic for him before, but everything seemed to be different about Eric. He took a simple task, like chewing, and turned it into something so much more. The way his lips pursed with each bite captured Zack's gaze, and the way he licked his lips had Zack shuddering. Even the way he cut the meat, with sure confident strokes, made Zack wonder.

When Eric lifted the last of the roast from the fire and tossed it out of the door, Zack sighed in relief. He thought he saw a flash of grey through the storm before the door slammed shut again and cut off the wind. The storm had hardly settled in the time he had been there, and the snow was so deep that he could no longer see his car from the window.

He followed Eric to the sink before sliding in front to take his place to do the dishes in the freshly warmed water. Something about it seemed routine. Eric provided the meat, and Zack would struggle it down and do the cleaning.

"I have an extra toothbrush if you want," said Eric as he strode the few steps to the other side of the cabin. Zack almost turned to look, but then he heard a zip and a rush of water that wasn't from a non-existent tap. Watching another man take a piss was not his idea of a good time, even if it gave him the opportunity to check out the prize.

He squinted at the sink as the light started to dim. It couldn't have been later than six o'clock, but Zack could barely keep his eyes open. He was not designed for manual labour unless he was on his knees, especially when he was sleep deprived from the night before.

"Thank you." He waited for the sound of feet padding across the floor before he dried his hands and turned to the bathroom, going through the bare basics of his nightly routine — minus his facial scrub, of course. He didn't want to have to boil the kettle yet again.

Eric tossed a few logs onto the fire, making the same rounds as the night before, minus his gross spiced milk. Anticipation burned in Zack's belly as darkness crept through the walls, bringing the chill and the wind of the storm. How long could the storm last before they were simply buried forever?

"Going to bed?" asked Zack, his stomach fluttering as Eric nodded. Maybe it was because his secret was out or because he knew Eric was maybe just a little bit like him, but the tension and awkwardness between them had started to dissolve. They were no longer two strangers.

Eric strode to the bed and pulled his shirt over his head, tossing it into the largest pile beside the bed. It was the pile that Zack had chosen from, and the one that had smelled most like Eric.

Zack felt his jaw drop as drool gathered at the corner of his lip. The man was stunning. His skin was smooth at the same time it was chiselled and hard. He could probably win one of the gameshows about ninjas and climb a rope one-handed. Someone with that much sculpting could lift their lover and put them onto their cock with no effort at all.

His chest was broad, with two defined pecs that had dusky pink nipples that appeared so kissable, even from a short distance. The nipples were peaked and surrounded by tiny hairs that shone in the flickering firelight. His waist narrowed, and the lines and ridges of his six-pack were on clear display. Zack had assumed that Eric was cut, from the way he felt through his thin tank, but he hadn't been quite ready for the reality of just how beautiful he was.

Two lines carved their way down to his clothed groin, disappearing beneath the low waistband where a few dark hairs peeked above the band. Even through his pants, he was large, but Zack craved to know what he really looked like. Was he cut? Did he curve to one side?

There was a white line on Eric's hip that curved over the bone and disappeared under the rise of his pants. Zack didn't realise that he was moving until his fingertips were on Eric's tanned skin, gliding over the pale scar. What he thought was one wound, were four parallel lines, each one starting with a jagged echo of torn flesh. Whatever had caused it had to have been massive.

"Are you sure that you aren't a werewolf?" asked Zack as he smoothed his finger down the path of the blemish, pausing at the obstructing waist band. The scars were nearly as thick as his finger, and he could only imagine how painful they must've been.

"I'm sure," said Eric, his voice deep like a tree falling in the bush with no one around. "I don't have any boxers or sleep pants. I usually sleep naked." A blush spread across his cheekbones and a shiver broke out where Zack had touched him.

"Same," said Zack, unable to tear his eyes away from the spot. Eric was so responsive, even from a simple touch. If only Zack could keep him from pulling away. "Not about the boxers, but about the sleeping in the nude. I just get tangled up if I have anything on. I was lucky last night because I didn't sleep. No strangulation risk." He smoothed over the lowest scar and dipped his finger inside the band, warmth teasing him. He wanted nothing more than to put his mouth on it and see how Eric would taste.

Eric cleared his throat and took a step away, his gaze cutting to the side and his blush deepening. Zack dropped his hands and he leaned back on his heels where he'd knelt. When had he ended up on the floor? He certainly hadn't meant to sit in such a precarious spot with Eric's cock only inches away from his mouth. He licked his lips, unable to tear his eyes away.

"Did you want me to turn around?" asked Zack, quirking one eyebrow as Eric's blush deepened even further. He felt their roles suddenly reverse, where he was the predator, and Eric was his blushing prey. "You know for someone as attractive as you are, you sure are shy. You positive you aren't a virgin?"

"I'm not," said Eric, his voice loud, even at a whisper. "Things just usually happen a lot different is all. No one's ever done something like that." He motioned to Zack's hand that had traced over the scars on his hip.

"No one has ever touched you?" Zack felt his heart still. If no one had ever taken their time with this man, then he was about to lose all faith in humanity. No one deserved that, especially not someone so attractive and painfully shy at heart. It was no wonder that Eric could be such an ass. He was probably hiding behind a layer of sarcastic confidence, just to avoid hurting.

No one had ever really taken their time with Zack either, but that was different. He had karma looking out for him. Eric had no one.

"Just not like that. Someone like me, it's different when this happens. It's not soft or sweet like you. It's…" He trailed off, casting his gaze up to the low ceiling. There was a cobweb dangling from the main beam, and it fluttered in the rising heat. "It's just different. Not bad, but different. Now turn around so I can get into bed."

Zack snorted, accepting the topic change and spinning around so he faced the fire. He heard the rustle of clothes, and the shuffle of the box spring against the floor as it took Eric's weight. He pulled at his socks, tossing them over his shoulder and hoping that he got close to the heaping pile. He would add laundry to tomorrow's list, not really knowing how he would do it without a machine.

He took a deep breath before he tugged at his own shirt, pulling it over his head and tossing it in the same spot. His stomach fluttered, but he tried to push the feeling away as he stood and fumbled with his pants. He hadn't bothered with boxers after his shower, and once his slacks slipped from his hips, he was naked. Eric had already kept his promise of keeping his eyes averted once, and Zack would have to trust him to do the same again.

Zack wasn't exactly self-conscious, and he was a wee bit sculpted, but deep down, he was painfully shy about letting anyone see the real him...the dangerous one. He could only look so good without going to the gym or doing any sort of manual labour except jerking off. He switched hands often, though, so he didn't get unbalanced. He skin was scar-free, with only a few sparse moles dotting it, and he kept himself well-groomed.

He turned to the bed, tossing his pants over to the pile. His socks and shirt had all missed, his shirt at the foot of the bed, and his socks on the fur cover.

The blanket shifted, and Zack's gaze shot up. There was a tent in the furs right at the level of Eric's groin, and he was blatantly staring at Zack's naked body. Eric didn't even have the decency to meet Zack's eyes but stayed firmly focussed on Zack's cock that was hanging loosely between his legs. It hardened under the scrutiny, fast enough to make his head spin. His skin flushed, the blush travelling up his groin and chest until he was certain that his face was painted rosy red.

He took two steps to the bed, his cock bouncing along like a wagging tail. His mind was quickly catching up, and he was more than ready to jump in. The air was cool against his flushed skin, but he was finally getting used to the permanent chill. And if the tent in the blanket counted for anything, at least Eric liked what he saw. That alone added a spring to Zack's step.

The correct thing to do would have been to cup himself to try to keep his decency, and shuffle under the blankets and face away. They were both tired, after all, and needed their rest. *Ha!*

But, since he'd never done the correct thing in his life, he did exactly what his cock wanted instead. He took the long way around the bed over to Eric's side, tugging at the blanket, which Eric had in an iron-tight grip.

"I'm not looking," Zack sang out as he slapped his hand over his eyes. He tugged blindly at the blanket and felt it give this time, revealing Eric's body to the room but not to him. His heart thudded as Zack let himself be revealed, darkness and all.

Feeling along the bed, with his eyes squinted tight, he crawled over Eric until he straddled his waist. They were only touching where Zack's inner thighs brushed Eric's hips, but it sent a shudder through him, nonetheless. With his eyes still shut he leaned down, searching for Eric's lips.

He missed.

His lips connected with the hard angle of Eric's defined jaw, his stubble scratching at the sensitive skin. He locked his elbows to hold himself aloft, so he didn't try to move too fast for Eric. He nibbled at his jaw, relishing in the gasp that was so close to his ear. Nosing his way up Eric's face, he finally found his lips and dove in.

It was heaven—if heaven included beautiful gay men with lithe muscles and the scent of pine on their skin. Or maybe it was hell. His heart certainly thought so with the way it was trying to beat its way out of his chest.

He licked his way into Eric's mouth, and the man gave way beneath him, letting him inside with a groan that could melt chocolate. Eric moved his strong hands to Zack's hips, bracing him and pulling him down to meet the rod of slick heat that rested against his own.

He moved deeper, twirling his tongue around Eric's as his cock twitched, sliding against the most perfectly soft skin that had ever been created. There was just the right amount of scratchy, wiry hair there, and it was enough to make the friction flawless.

Tilting his hips, he lifted and rolled, sliding their cocks together until Eric's cockhead tickled the base of his balls. Eric jerked him down a second later, lining up perfectly with the crevice between Zack's cheeks. He slid between the sweat-damp tunnel that Zack's cheeks created, zipping against his hole until the head of Eric's cock glanced his most sensitive part.

"Fuck," Zack cried out, his eyes snapping open as he sat up, rocking back against Eric's cock with everything he had. He loved getting his cock wet and would take a blow job any day of the week, but his hole was where the party was at. He was sensitive, and tight enough that even the littlest penetration had the potential to get him off. And he loved the feel of a cock rubbing back there, threatening to breech but holding back.

Eric wasn't even threatening, with how still he was holding himself. His eyes were partially closed, with his lips parted and glistening. His flush had deepened, spreading over the bridge of his nose and down his chest. He was fucking beautiful.

Eric stayed nearly still except for the involuntary twitches that he made every time Zack brushed against the head of his slick cock. It was his arms that were doing all the work, and Zack's abdominals, as he rolled his ass like a porn star.

"Do you have anything?" asked Zack as he panted from the exertion. His thighs were burning, but he spread his hands over Eric's chest, pushing past the burn as he revelled in the smooth skin. He wanted Eric inside him now — or ten minutes ago — whichever came first.

"What do you mean?" Eric growled, as he snapped his hips up once, nearly breeching Zack's hole as he seemed to lose his semblance of control. Zack let out a startled yell, more from surprise than the zing of pain that flickered at the base of his spine. Eric's cock felt absolutely massive, and there was no way he would be able to take it unprepared.

"You know — condoms, lube, cock rings, dildos, handcuffs and blindfolds…that kind of stuff." Zack rolled back again, locking his gaze with Eric's. His eyes really were just like liquid gold, ready to be poured into a jeweller's mould.

"Oh… No. Why would we need that? You won't get pregnant." Eric's brows pinched in confusion, and his kiss-reddened lips quirked.

Zack stuttered to a halt as his plans for an amazing night burned into ashes. "You're kidding, right?" He glared down at Eric, suddenly hating the cock that was twitching between his cheeks — a cock that he couldn't have without protection, a cock that would feel so good to take bare but also might be carrying a northern version of herpes.

"No," said Eric, his hands stilling and his lips parting in a pant.

"You have got to be fucking kidding me," said Zack as he lifted himself off Eric's hips, throwing the blanket back over him and stomping to the opposite side of the bed. "I finally get you naked and get you to stop pushing me away, and you don't even have any condoms. Thank you, Karma. Payback's a bitch." He cursed at the ceiling and the voyeuristic spider that was watching them from above. "And, of course, I left all of mine behind in my rush to get out of my last place. The cherry on the cake is that we are in the middle of fucking nowhere with enough snow to start the next ice age outside the door. I imagine it'll be days before we can get to a store."

He threw himself onto the bed, facing away from Eric and pulled the blanket up to his shoulder. His cock was still throbbing, neglected and rejected between his legs, but that came second to the pure rage that had followed the most epic cock block of his life.

"Why are you yelling?" asked Eric, his voice soft and tentative. The blanket shifted, and Zack felt a wave of heat at his back as he moved closer.

"Because I'm fucking horny, but we aren't fucking without protection. I don't care how hot you are or how much I want you. And my balls are already blue as fuck. They might just shrivel up and die after this."

Zack pulled the blanket tighter in an attempt to keep his hands to himself. He was shaking with the effort.

"In my defence, I only promised you a kiss." Eric's breath fluttered against the back of his neck, crumbling Zack's anger with those few whispered words. Eric reached over him, touching the point of his jaw and gently persuading him to turn around. The moment he did, lips were on his own, taking his breath away.

He rolled onto his back, cupping Eric's jaw and pulling him down. The blushing Eric was gone, and a man with raw lust and longing was in his place. He devoured Zack, carving into his mouth with his tongue and sucking the gasps from his lips.

There was no hesitation, only lust, as Eric slid over his body, settling between his vulnerable thighs without ever removing his lips. The man kissed as if he were starving…as if he were wild, and Zack was the only source of nourishment that he'd seen for days. Zack could hardly keep up, and he wasn't sure if he even wanted to try.

Their teeth clacked as Eric ground down, his hot cock leaving a wet streak along Zack's groin and belly. The man was so hard, and every place he touched sent another wave of warmth over Zack. But it was more than just heat and lust. There was something beneath his skin, buzzing and making his hair stand on end. With each touch, it grew louder, until it was nearly consuming him.

Zack sucked in a lungful of air as Eric finally released him, dropping lower to bite at his jaw and skim his teeth along his neck. The bites edged along the line of pain but weren't hard enough to leave bruises or break skin. Only enough to make Zack feel completely and utterly claimed.

Eric seemed to have an obsession with his neck, kissing along the ridge of his jugular on each side, then back down to the U-shape between his clavicles, biting along the bone and sucking the skin. The sucks were hard enough to bring blood to the surface, and he knew it would leave him collared for a week.

"Fuck, don't stop," said Zack as he gripped Eric's shoulders, unsure if he wanted to pull the man up to his mouth or push him down to what he hoped was his next destination.

"I won't stop," said Eric, his voice so low that it was nothing more than a growl. His shoulders flexed under Zack's hands as he palmed at Zack's ass, spreading his cheeks wide enough so that his blunt cock could slip between them again. His cock dribbled a steady bead of pre-cum, slicking the way in a few thrusts.

Zack shuddered as the blunt head pressed against his entrance again, bumping and jostling the sensitive surface. It felt like he would be breeched at any moment. All it would take was one wrong angle and a too-strong thrust.

"Don't," Zack groaned as his rim was expertly stroked by a cock that was hard enough to pound nails. If it pierced him, like it was threatening to do, he would tear for sure. Not to mention, there would be nothing between them, and nothing to slick the way but what his body had to offer. He was terrified and thrilled with the idea at the same time, and his cock throbbed violently against his stomach, forgotten and ignored.

"I won't mount you, Zack," said Eric, panting against Zack's chest before closing his lips around his nipple.

Mount? What the fuck?

Zack arched into the touch, gripping hard enough to bruise. Teeth grazed the peaked bud, insistent and terrifying with how good it felt.

"I already told you. I'm not that easy." Eric's hips stuttered, and he bit down on the bud between his teeth, bringing another gasp to Zack's lips.

"You could have fooled me," said Zack, moving his hands to Eric's hair and twining his fingers through the strands. "You're the one who got naked first."

Eric let out another growl, the sound rumbling low in his chest, sending the first pang of real fear into Zack's belly. The teeth against his nipple seemed to sharpen, grinding the sensitive peak.

"I want to bite you," said Eric, pushing himself up on his hands so he hovered over Zack, his hair like a halo draped around them. He looked away and his eyes almost glowed in the semi-darkness. "Let me suck you. I want to taste you."

"What? Ah, no, thank you," said Zack, gripping Eric's hair like a handle to hold him away from his precious junk. "You can't say you want to bite me, then go for my cock." His dick pulsed on his belly, unaware of the very real danger it was in.

"I want to bite you here," said Eric, pulling against Zack's grip as if it were nothing. His mouth settled against Zack's neck, just above his shoulder, in the spot that Eric seemed borderline obsessed with. "Your cock is the last thing I'd ever want to hurt, and I think it will keep me from biting you if I just get to taste you. Please, let me taste you." He took a shuddering breath, and at Zack's shaky nod, lowered himself.

The first tentative lick had Zack biting back a shout and gripping the hair in his hands hard. The man's mouth was absolute sin, but this was something beyond. This could not be compared to any of his previous blows, and Eric had barely started.

"You're circumcised," said Eric as he licked another stripe over the sensitive head, lingering on the tiny moist slit. "I think I like it." He circled around the head with his tongue, dipping down to suck at the small amount of loose skin at the underside of his shaft.

Zack glanced down, realising that he hadn't even seen Eric's cock yet. He had only imagined how big and beautiful it was. His view was blocked by Eric's reddened lips stretching over him.

Zack cried out, thrusting his hips into the air. Eric's hand clamped on his gyrating hips, forcing him down into the mattress.

"You taste good. Sweeter than I expected, but the darkness is here, too. I can taste it all over my tongue." He closed his lips over the head and sucked.

Zack's eyes rolled back into his head as he momentarily forgot how to breathe. Eric's mouth was so hot and tight, better than any part of anyone that he'd ever fucked. And the suction the man was giving him, would put a Dyson to shame.

The warmth and the slickness dropped down his cock until he was all the way inside the moist cavern, the head of his cock settled neatly into Eric's throat. Eric blinked up at him through dark lashes that shimmered in the firelight. He didn't even have tears in his eyes.

"No gag reflex, fuck," said Zack, wishing that he could say the same for himself. Sometimes he gagged just from brushing his teeth, and cock was another matter. He could take three inches into his mouth max before he had to pull off. Anything farther, and he would tap out. Only one person had tried to push him beyond that limit, and they had paid for it.

Eric bobbed his head, somehow keeping the suction up while flicking his tongue along the vein on the underside of Zack's cock. Time seemed to slow around them. Every part of Zack was focussed on the hands on his hips, heavy and warm, and the scratch of Eric's stubble on the inside of his thighs. Eric's hair tickled his groin as it fell forwards to obscure the beautiful gold eyes from view. It was too much.

He came harder than he thought possible, his hips jerking and his sac clenching as he emptied himself into Eric's throat. The man groaned as if Zack were giving him a taste of thousand-dollar wine, and he swallowed every last drop.

When he pulled off, Zack was near boneless on the bed, his chest heaving and his mind swimming. For a full minute, he stared at the flickering ceiling and wondered how he could have missed out on something like this in his life—something so good that it literally took his breath away and left his cock so sensitive that the rest of him felt numb.

Eric pulled himself off Zack, rolling onto his back next to him with his chest still heaving and the blanket tented over his groin. Groggily, Zack reached for him, intending to do his best to return the favour but knowing he would probably have to settle for a handy. He hadn't seen Eric's cock up close and personal quite yet, but it felt like he wouldn't even be able to fit it comfortably between his lips, let alone take it his determined three inches.

He gripped the blanket, ready to pull it off his prize when Eric's hand closed over his wrist. He looked up into the gold gaze, wondering where he had gone wrong. Eric had drawn his brows together and there was a strained frown on his lips as he slowly moved Zack's hand away from him.

"Don't."

"I'm sorry," said Zack, moving away faster than his beating heart. He raised his hands automatically, as if he were surrendering to a police officer. *What did I do wrong?* He was only trying to do the polite thing and make sure Eric didn't go to bed with blue balls, either.

"Don't apologise," said Eric, shaking his head. The frown on his lips deepened. "I'm just not ready for that yet." He shrugged and looked away, but the tension in his muscles didn't ease. If anything, it wound tighter. "Just go to sleep."

Zack lowered his hands to the bed, his mouth opening and closing a few times before he snapped it shut. There was something that Eric wasn't telling him, and it had nothing to do with him not being ready.

He scooted over to the edge of the bed, facing away and glaring across the room at the crackling fire. He heard a soft sigh behind him, then a shuffle of the blanket.

"Can I hold you?" asked Eric, his voice much closer than Zack expected. He nodded, not trusting himself to speak. His eyes burned from unshed tears from the powerful rejection, and the low that always came for him after an orgasm. The heat at his back settled it some, allowing him to slide his eyes shut. He fell asleep with a soft breath on the back of his neck and a hard cock nestled between the cheeks of his ass.

Chapter Eight

The sun somehow seemed brighter than usual as it peeked through the half-covered windows. It took him a moment to realise that it was quieter than it had been in days. There was no wind battering the old panes of glass, and the snow had finally stopped its incessant whirling.

Zack was warm, even with the fire burned down to nothing more than a pile of grey ash with a heart of red coals. Heat radiated from behind him, naked skin sticking to his. A fluttering breath brushed against the back of his neck, making him tingle and encouraging his morning wood to life. Nestled between his cheeks was the largest cock he'd ever had the privilege of touching. Even now, as Eric slept, it was nearly overwhelming with its presence.

But something was missing. There was no buzzing beneath his skin, something that he hadn't even noticed until Eric had named it. *His darkness.* It was…gone — or at least quiet, settled deep in his bones where it couldn't harm anyone.

His neck was heavy and stiff as he tried to move, as if something were pulling him back. An ache sharpened just below the base of his skull. He reached back, his fingers threading through Eric's hair.

A growl split the air, so close that it rumbled directly into his ear, and strong arms tightened around his waist. They were so solid that they threatened to push the air from his lungs. He fought to keep still, remembering what Eric had done the last time he'd struggled.

"Are you biting me?" Zack yelled out into the quiet room, shooting an elbow back and striking Eric somewhere along his chest. A zing travelled up his arm, like he'd struck solid metal and not a sleeping body. Eric grunted, his teeth pinching harder at the back of Zack's neck, hard enough that he arched and cried out.

"Shit," a mumbling voice grumbled against him a moment before he was released. "Sorry."

Zack slapped a hand to the back of his neck, half expecting the slick surface to come away red. There was only a glint of saliva on his hand and a hint of soreness. He shot another elbow back, bracing himself for the impact this time.

"Why the fuck did you bite me?" Zack asked, wriggling in Eric's grasp, and only succeeding in rutting against the cock between his cheeks. He paused as it nudged his rim, lighting up his nerves in the most delicious way.

"Sorry... I was dreaming." Eric gripped Zack hard, pulling him back against his chest and humping him. The man's voice was slurred, as if he hadn't really woken up yet. Zack peeked back over his shoulder.

Eric's eyes were closed, and his lashes fluttered against his cheeks.

"I dreamt you were trying to get away. I had you all ready for me—ready to mount—and you wanted me to chase you. I caught you," Eric continued to mumble, his teeth grazing over Zack's neck again.

Zack felt himself flush bright at Eric's words. *Mount?* He'd said it the night before, too, but Zack had let it slide in the moment. What the hell *was* he? The tally for werewolf kept getting higher, even as Eric denied it.

"What are you dreaming about now?" Zack asked quietly, rolling his hips. He tried to reach back to grasp Eric's cock and get his first feel, but they were just too close together to get the right angle. He didn't want to get bitten again if he tried to put room between them, either.

"Mmm-mm," said Eric, nuzzling close as his voice dropped between layers of sleep. "You're keeping so still for me with your ass in the air, all ready for me to show you who you belong to." His hips thrust forwards hard, nudging Zack's entrance harshly but not sinking inside. The man was just too wide and too blunt. "You're so tight." He growled then his teeth were back, biting savagely into Zack's neck.

He felt the moment that Eric broke skin and the heat that flared straight to his groin like some kind of drug. His mind blurred, and everything pinpointed to the spot on the back of his neck. He didn't know what was happening, but he couldn't bring himself to care.

Zack let out a strangled yelp as he was immobilised, Eric's cock coming closer and closer to breeching him. His own cock twitched, on board from the very beginning and not worrying about the consequences of no prep and no condom.

He thrust his hand back, fumbling between them until he found Eric's cock. It was heavy and rock hard in his hand, harder than he could have imagined, and something about it felt *off*.

Eric hissed as Zack grabbed just under the head and pointed his cock up so it would slide harmlessly along his tailbone and not between his cum-slick cheeks.

Eric grunted, slamming his hips forwards as his cock found purchase and heat where Zack had guided it. Zack reached for Eric's arms, holding on for the ride and loving every second of it. The man was wild, even in his sleep, and hit Zack's primal kink on the head. He was glad he had repositioned, though, or else he would have been broken and bleeding from the brutal thrust.

Eric's teeth tightened until Zack was sure he would be bruised and bleeding for days, and the man's hips stuttered against his ass. Wetness coated his lower back and cheeks, dripping down to the bed.

There was a lot — enough to make Zack instantly crave another shower and dread his plans for doing laundry. It was also hot as hell to be marked with Eric's cum.

"Ugh." Zack reached down, gripping himself in a tight hold, and pulling three times before his toes curled, and he splattered against his palm and the underside of the blanket that somehow still clung to them. He groaned long and low, rutting back into the mess and forwards into his palm, even as he became too sensitive.

The arms around him clenched tighter than a compound bow as Eric's entire body went still. His teeth retracted for a second time, and Zack let out a sigh of relief, flopping his head down and forwards to stretch out his spine. It popped and cracked as he rolled his shoulders. It didn't hurt as much as he'd thought, but it burned something fierce.

"It's okay," said Zack, squeezing Eric's hand before relaxing into the hold. "That was amazing." It was probably the best spooning experience that he'd ever had, which was a little bit sad. Eric hadn't even been awake for it, but the man had been dreaming about him, so it still had to count.

"I didn't hurt you?" Eric nosed against Zack's neck, blowing over the bruises and making every hair on Zack's body stand up. "I was asleep, but not really. I was here, but I wasn't." He hadn't relaxed his hold and Eric was oddly still.

"I guess it's a little too late to ask for consent, eh?" Zack said, his stomach dropping as his brain caught up. He hadn't asked for consent, but how was he supposed to when Eric was asleep?

"I touched your dick...just a little. I know you said you weren't ready for it, but you were trying to break down a door that was not ready to open." His slowing heart picked up when Eric didn't reply but sighed against his neck. "It's a nice dick by the way—at least by the head. Can't tell you about the rest of it because I couldn't reach." Zack clenched his eyes shut waited to get kicked out on his ass in the snow.

Instead, Eric relaxed and let out a soft chuckle. "I tried to mount you, came all over your back and you're worried about touching my dick?" Eric snorted, rolling away and rustling on the other side of the bed. "You have my consent, past, future and present. I'll just try to be awake for it next time."

He was already clothed by the time Zack rolled over, cum smearing on the fitted sheet. Zack lay back and let out a soft sigh. *What the hell is going on?*

* * * *

Zack grumbled as Eric easily flipped a piece of meat in the cast-iron pan that was perched on the coals. His own piece had somehow slipped in the grease and ended up sinking into a pile of ashes. It wasn't his fault that he was a klutz when it came to something as nerve-racking as cooking over a fire. Give him any stove, and he could cook anything to perfection, but open flames? *No thank you.* He was already missing the hair off one of his hands, and now his breakfast was ruined.

"It's good for you," Eric snickered as he watched Zack dip his breakfast into a bowl of cool water. It sucked the heat and flavour from the meat, leaving a soggy, bland mess behind.

"It can't be that hard to get a stove out here," said Zack, shaking his head. "I mean, they make wood stoves *for* places like this, and it would be so much safer than cooking over an open flame." He'd tried bacon in the barbecue once, only to nearly burn his mother's house down when he had looked away to admire her very athletic neighbour who had been raking leaves while shirtless. It had been completely worth it, especially when the neighbour saw the flames and came to his rescue.

"I usually eat it raw, to be honest. I only cook it when I want to mix things up—or if I have company that prefers it cooked." Eric swirled the pan, gripping the hot handle with a thin oven mitt.

"Gross," said Zack, sticking his tongue out and holding his breath as he shoved the meat into his mouth, chewing a bare minimum of times before swallowing. "Let me educate you on the finer points of not getting food poisoning. Please heat all meat to an internal temperature of one-hundred-and sixty-five-degrees, so you don't spend the next week puking your guts out."

Eric shrugged. "It doesn't matter for me. I don't get sick. I *can't*. One of the perks of being what I am."

"Which is?" Zack raised one brow and smirked, not expecting an answer in the least. He should have asked the man while he was still half-asleep in hump-land, but his cock got the better of him. The suspense was terrible.

Eric took a deep breath, tugging a lock of hair as he looked down into the flames. His hair shone with so many colours, the blond mixed with brown making him look more mature, and the fiery red making him look like a hot head.

"I'm a d —" His voice cut off as he snapped his head up to look at the door. The pan tilted into the flames, sending up a burst of flames as the grease dribbled over hot coals. The food was ruined, burnt black in a split second of carelessness, but Eric didn't even seem to care. He was already lifting himself to his feet, stalking to the door while padding soundlessly on the ground. His head tilted back as he scented the air.

"Eric?" asked Zack, shuffling away from the spitting flames. A deep pit had settled into his stomach the moment that Eric had dropped the pan. It was the same feeling he had every time something was about to go wrong.

The buzzing under his skin was back, as if it had never left in the first place. It was like running a humming razor over his skin, each vibration penetrating into his muscle and bone. *His darkness.*

"Stay here," said Eric, looking over his shoulder as his eyes flashed bright. His lips were pulled back, showing his teeth that looked suddenly sharper. He gripped the door latch, flicking it open and pushing the door wide. Wearing nothing but a T-shirt and shorts, he walked out into the cold, letting the door slam behind him.

The feeling in Zack's gut worsened, and for a moment he thought he might vomit the slippery meat that he'd just swallowed. His mouth went dry.

He crept to the door, grabbing his shoes and coat before slipping them on. He never was good at following directions, especially when he could feel the danger like a flashing neon light.

He lifted the latch slowly, pulling the door open a few centimetres and peering out through the crack. Cold air trickled against his face, but the wind had calmed. A wonderland of white shone back at him, cutting through the perpetual dimness of the cabin.

An unfamiliar voice drifted through the door.

"Hey, Coy-Boy," said the voice, with a taunting edge that put Zack on full alert. "Why don't you invite us in, and we can get reacquainted?" Zack opened the door wider, peering out into the glistening landscape.

Eric stood with his back to the door, halfway between the cabin and the tree line. His shoulders were tense and high, and his hands were clenched into fists. His hair fluttered around his shoulders, but he paid it no mind. With his bare feet and his aggressive stance, he had never looked more wild or threatening.

There were three people beyond him, all of them clothed in very little, or nothing, in the one man's case. They had to be lunatics, or something unnatural, to be standing there without feeling the snow beneath their feet. Their skin was bronze in way that was so similar to Eric's, but that was where their similarities ended.

They were big, not so much taller than Eric, as they were wider. They had the bulk of three men who had made it their life's passion to abuse steroids. Their shoulders were wide enough that Zack doubted they would even fit through the door, and their bodies were taut with aggression. He wouldn't want to face them in an alley alone.

Zack tried not to drop his gaze, but he couldn't help himself. They shouldn't have been mostly naked if he wasn't supposed to look.

He'd always heard that men who took steroids had shrivelled cocks with no balls to speak of. That was definitely not the case from what he could see. The naked man was hung like a horse, his cock hanging half-hard in the cold winter air.

"Go, Jared," said Eric, his voice nothing more than a growl as he glared at the naked intruder. He moved one shoulder down unnaturally and a drop of blood dribbled onto the snow. Zack followed the blood to Eric's hand, where his nails had sharpened into claws, cutting through the thick skin of his palms.

Jared, the biggest of the three, took a step away from the trees and into the light. The sun glistened against his bronze skin, momentarily taking Zack's breath away. He was breath-taking. But his eyes—his eyes were the black pools of a soulless ghoul.

"That's not very nice of you, Coy-Boy, especially after last time. I might just have to come up there and teach you a lesson…teach you some manners. Or maybe that's what you want?" The man's cock twitched as he took another step forwards. "Last time you were begging for it — and begging me to stay." The man let out a cruel laugh, shaking his head, even as Eric let out a steady stream of low growls.

Zack had one-hundred percent heard enough. If there were two things he absolutely detested, it was manipulators and rapists. He'd never had any guilt when his curse had tried to take them out.

"I think he asked you to go away," said Zack, pushing the door all the way open. Three sets of black eyes turned to him, and Eric's shoulders drooped, his hands dropping open.

"I thought I smelled a tasty snack on the wind. You finally found someone you can top, Coy-Boy?" said Jared, taking a step towards Zack and tilting his head back to scent the air.

Zack tried not to shudder as the wind ruffled his thin jacket, pushing ice where heat had been. He raised his chin and stood as tall as his five-foot-nine body would go. Luckily, the cabin was a step up from the ground, so Jared had to look up to him, even if it was only by a bit.

"Ugh, a human? Really, Coy-Boy? Even I would never stoop so low, and I've had your sloppy ass." He took another step, his black eyes widening as he took a deep breath. "I can see the appeal, though. There's something a bit exotic about this one."

The man stopped just short of the step, his eyes almost level with Zack's. Those soulless orbs drew him in like a black hole in space. He tried to hold his gaze and not look away, but he couldn't help it when his eyes dropped down between the man's legs. His cock looked even bigger up-close, although a bit strange-looking — but it had lost its appeal.

"You like what you see, little treat?" The man let out a smile that was all teeth. They looked too big for his jaw, the shape angular and strange.

"I've seen bigger," said Zack, just able to keep the tremor from his voice. He didn't have to say that the bigger cock had been on an actual horse at his grandfather's farm. His grandfather had owned a dozen stallions that he studded out, and he charged a pretty penny for it, too. Zack was still scarred from the day that his grandfather had made him watch a *live covering*.

"You like them big, don't you, little treat? I could show you a good time. I'd never leave you wanting." The two other men at the tree line were closing in, flanking them on either side.

"It would be hard to leave me wanting, seeing as I don't want it in the first place." Zack shook his head, stepping right up to the edge of the step and glowering an inch above Jared. "Eric has everything I'll ever need and more. You can take your useless tree trunk and fuck off."

"You're going to regret that," said Jared, his black eyes narrowing and his massive hands curling into fists. They were close enough to touch him, and close enough that those hands could rip Zack's throat out. He looked powerful enough to be able to do it.

A blur of tan and grey grabbed Zack's attention, pulling his gaze back to the tree line. Bounding amongst the deep snow was the coyote, his yellow eyes wide and foam dribbling from his curled lips. The snarl from his throat caught the attention of all three black-eyed men, but not before he was lunging at the smallest of the three.

"No!" Eric screamed, his terrified voice echoing through the clearing. "Stop, please." Blood dribbled from his hands as he fell to his knees in the deep snow. A wail came from his throat that chilled Zack to the bone. He sounded defeated, utterly and completely, even though the coyote had already taken down one of the intruders, lying atop them in the snow. With the three of them working together, it should have been easy to take out the other two intruders.

Zack's stomach dropped as a yelp followed seconds after Eric's plea. Blood painted the snow, but it wasn't from the downed intruder. There was a crack of bone and a tearing sound, before the coyote was thrown an inhuman distance. Its crumpled, bleeding body smashed into a nearby tree before landing limp on the ground, sinking beneath the top layer of snow that was already soaked with blood.

The intruder stood from where the coyote had pinned him. Zack expected bite wound or claw marks to be marring the tanned skin, but it was pristine. His black eyes were wide, and a cruel smirk had carved its way onto his lips. His breath was coming shallow and fast, but it looked like it was from excitement and not exertion.

Eric had crumpled onto the ground, his face in his hands as sobs racked his body. His head was shaking back and forth in either denial or a plea not to be the next one.

For the first time in Zack's life, he felt a twinge of fear for his own well-being. He'd always been afraid for others but not for himself. He'd been safe with his curse looking out for him, but now, seeing such a powerful man crumple to nothing, he was terrified.

Jared let out a braying laugh before he turned to Zack, an ugly sneer on his face. Zack took a stuttering step back, his knees going weak.

"Someone is going to have to pay for that," he said, his smile widening to show off too-large teeth. "We would have just had our fun and been on our way, but if you think you can attack one of us and get away with it, well, others might start to get the wrong idea."

Eric's shoulders shook as he looked at Jared. Blood had smeared over his face from the open wounds on his hands, mixing with tears and trailing down to his chin.

"I'll go with you," said Zack, taking the step back to the edge. His gut was a trembling mess, but he couldn't take the look on Eric's face. The man was...defeated.

A grin burst across Jared's face, and he let out a laugh that echoed around the clearing. "I have a feeling you might be something special. Maybe a little demon blood in you, but not like this pathetic half-blood here."

Zack's blood turned to ice.

Demon.

Chapter Nine

Was that what Eric had been trying to tell him? It didn't make any sense. Demons were from way down south, where your soul went to burn to ashes….at least that's what his mother used to say to him. He may not have been a believer, but every myth or tale had to start from something.

Demons were something malicious. They weren't beautiful — or shy or nervous. They couldn't be. They were just…evil.

Eric's shoulders slumped, and his gaze dropped to the ruffled snow. Tears ran freely from his face as he mouthed the same words over and over. "I'm sorry."

"Come on, Jared," said one of the flanking men. "Can't we have a little fun first? I mean, before we hand him over." He strode forwards, stepping by Eric as if the man didn't even exist anymore. "You promised us some fun."

"No," said Zack, not moving from his spot on the step. He looked away from Eric, pushing his shock away to be dealt with later. If he could accept a werewolf, then he could accept a demon.

The cold seeped into his toes, and he was sure they would be blue and frozen soon. His hands were freezing, too, but he kept them at his sides.

"I'm not sure you understand, little treat—"

"I said *no*," said Zack, cutting Jared off with an enjoyable amount of relish. "And if you don't like it, then push me. Fucking try it." An energy zinged under his skin as he said it, so familiar and dark that his terror was almost automatic. This time he was ready, and he was determined to embrace it, his past be damned.

Everything changed between the rhythmic strokes of two heartbeats. The darkness thrummed until it singed every nerve as it tried to escape. Usually, he would clamp down on it, running before his fear took over. This time Zack let it go, glaring at the man who threatened him.

Jared reached for him, his hand outstretched and aimed at Zack's neck. The tendons along his arm bulged and he lifted his lips into a snarl—one that promised pain and suffering.

A flash brighter than anything he'd ever seen blinded him at the same time a rattling roar burst against his ear drums. Every hair on his body sprang upright as an all-mighty crack sounded in the air. Heat sizzled against his skin and crashed into Jared with so much force that the echo of it slammed Zack back and into the cabin. The advancing men were pushed to the ground from the same force, and Eric tumbled, his face dunking into the snow.

It was lightning, so close that he could hear the sizzle as it struck Jared's body and turned him into nothing more than a smoking corpse. Zack retched as he trembled from the proximity to the charge and the smell that was quickly overwhelming him. The sky was nearly cloudless, but it had come from nowhere, like an angel bent on revenge.

As quickly as it came, it disappeared into nothingness, only the ringing in his ears and the heat on his skin evidence of its brief existence.

The front step was painted with ash and the lowest portion of the step smouldered. His nerves were shot and shaky as if he'd touched his hand to a cattle fence and left it there for hours. The lights dancing in his eyes blocked everything from view, and his ears buzzed, leaving him alone with nothing but the sound of his own thoughts.

His senses came back slowly—his vision first, then his hearing. There was a groan from somewhere out in the snow, and he tried to lift his head, but it was no use. His limbs were shaking, and he felt weaker than an hour-old deer trying to stand for the first time. His heart was pounding, too, in an irregular beat that made his chest throb.

He heard yelling, and screams, but they faded beneath the blood rushing through his veins and the smell in the air. He retched again, tasting his terrible breakfast for a second time before it slid from his body.

A face came into view, still smeared with blood and smudged with the sooty aftermath of the strike. Tear-stained gold looked down at him as Eric lifted him from the cold porch. The door screeched open then slammed shut with a wave of warmth.

"Where?" Zack tried to ask where the intruders had gone—the ones that had dared threaten to rape him and his friend. He was only able to get one scratchy word out before he started to cough, his heart beating wildly.

"They ran. They were afraid." Eric answered slowly as he lowered Zack onto something soft. Eric's eyes were wide, his nostrils flaring as he breathed deep, his pupils mere pinpoints.

Zack gripped the fabric beneath him that was still encrusted with the cum from their lovemaking. It would have been comforting if it wasn't so gross at the same time.

"My chest." Zack managed as his breath stuttered, and his heart pounded even fiercer. It felt like it might break out of his chest if it beat any harder. His head was starting to swim, even as he tried to focus on the dangling spiderweb above the bed.

"Do you trust me?" asked Eric, his voice hard. His chest was rising with rapid breaths too, and his hands were shaking where they touched Zack.

"No," said Zack honestly. He took another breath. "I don't trust anyone." Not the family or friends he had cut ties with—and not himself. He thought he could trust his curse to keep him safe, but he certainly didn't feel safe. He felt like he was one beat away from a heart attack.

"If I don't help you, you're going to die. Let me help you." A hand pressed against Zack's chest, and he struggled against the grip. There was something wrong with it...something unnatural. It pulled at the buzz under his skin, drawing it forth like a hair that was stretched too far, destined to snap.

He could feel it. His *darkness*. If he concentrated hard enough, he might be able to reach out and touch it as it hovered between them. It was so warm, like coffee that was the perfect temperature, or a heated blanket wrapped around his body.

Eric's fingers were clawed and covered with thick, soft hair that tickled the naked skin on his arm. He should've been afraid of it, and of Eric's demonic side, but he wasn't. He'd never felt safer in his life.

"Help me," said Zack, swallowing a gulp of air. Something shifted in the air as soon as he said it. There was no sound, no smell and the hairs on his arms didn't stand up, but something was *off*.

He pried his eyes open, needing to see the reassuring gold as his heart settled in his chest. His darkness wound between them, an invisible cloud that twined their bodies and souls together. Eric's black, empty gaze met his.

Chapter Ten

"A demon?" Zack pulled the blanket around his shoulders and shuffled closer to the fire. The blanket had been washed, thank God, and had the fresh scent of pine instead of crusted cum coating it. It was still slightly damp, but he had no other choice. The cabin was lacking in most essential things, including Wi-Fi and extra blankets.

"And you have some sort of magical powers?" He looked over at Eric, who had slid to the floor beside him, leaving a few feet as a buffer. His black eyes had faded to gold the moment he had released Zack's chest.

"It's not magic," said Eric with a shake of his head. His long hair brushed over his shoulders, still singed and smelling of ozone. "Demons are connected to the earth in the same way that were-animals are connected to the moon. There was energy trapped in your body and wreaking havoc on your heart. I grounded you."

"Huh," said Zack as he bit his lip. "You're like the ground wire on an extension cord. But I thought you said you were worse than a werewolf? How is being connected to the earth worse?" His mind buzzed as he tried to keep up. Werewolves, demons and fucking magic. *What the hell have I ever done to deserve this kind of drama?*

"I draw my strength from something I can touch and hold in my hands. Were-animals can only gaze up at the moon and long for it. They'll never be as powerful, and most of them are unstable. Some can't even keep a human shape, and others simply get trapped as animals."

Something clicked in Zack's mind as Eric said that. "The coyote?" It had seemed unnatural when Zack had first seen it, with yellow eyes that were intimidatingly steady — and the way it had gone for his throat, just like Eric had, not to kill, but to claim.

"Is my half-brother." Eric let out a sigh, his hands shaking in the firelight. "He's one of the trapped ones. It would take something profound to release him from that state, but a part of him is still there...and a part of him remembers me." Eric had left Zack's side as soon as his heart had calmed, but the coyote had already disappeared from the bloodied snow with his staggering paw prints leading into the forest.

"I'm sorry," said Zack, his stomach dropping. "How did it happen?" He pictured an epic battle, like the one that had occurred on the front step of the cabin.

"It just did." Eric's gaze was steady on the flickering fire. "He changed as the moon rose into the wild beast that he is. He had no control, only hunger. When it fell, he stayed as a coyote. That was forty years ago. He still stays close and comes by for a meal when he's hungry."

Zack remembered when Eric had thrown their leftovers out into the woods.

"They said you were a half-blood. Does that mean you could get trapped, too?" For some reason the idea of that terrified him. Eric was the only one who seemed to be immune to his curse, and he didn't want to lose that.

Something flickered in his chest, softer than the fire but just as warm. He pulled the blanket tighter, trying to keep his shivering at bay.

Eric shook his head. "My mother is a were-coyote. She's Jake's mom, too, but we have different fathers. His is dead, has been from the moment after Jake was conceived. She met my father shortly after and fell in love with him. A few years later they had me. The demon half from my father makes me stable. I'll never be trapped."

"I'm not going to even ask how that works," said Zack, looking down at his hands. His nailbeds were tinted grey and his fingers ached, as if the lightening had come from his hands and not from the sky.

Eric's hands had healed much faster than his own. The wounds on his palms had long since closed, the scars faded and the blood flaked away to nothing. It was another touch of magic that Zack filed away. He couldn't face it today, not all at once, while his chest still ached.

"There were enough similarities between my parents that they could match. My father? His line is as old as they come. He's something like a dire wolf, only older and much larger." Eric continued to speak, even as Zack's mind slowed, sluggishly trying to absorb Eric's words.

Zack had heard of dire wolves. They were massive creatures that nightmares were made of. They'd died out long before, but people still told stories about them when their bones were unearthed. To imagine something like that existing in the modern world was more than he could fathom.

"You seem to be taking this all very well," said Eric, his lips turning up in a small smile. "Not that I'm complaining, but you should be afraid of me, Zack. You should be terrified." His smile dropped away behind a curtain of mottled hair.

"You are the first thing that actually makes sense in my life," said Zack, pushing the blanket away and reaching for Eric. That was the *only* thing he was sure about. "You are the first one that I actually feel safe with—"

"You aren't safe with me," said Eric, cutting Zack off and jerking away. "I'm dangerous, Zack. I can hardly even control myself around you. I want to claim you and bite you so that *they* will know you are mine. I want it so bad that my teeth ache."

"I didn't say that you were safe to be around, Eric." Zack snarled, throwing himself at Eric and holding him tight when he tried to move away. He knew Eric could break his grip easily, but he had had enough. He couldn't take another rejection...not now.

"I meant that you were safe *from* me. I don't think you understand how much of a relief it is that, for once, I don't have to be afraid. I don't have to worry that I'll let my guard down, and you'll end up with a piano on your head. You are safe, and for the first time in my life, I feel free."

Silence hung in the air, his words resounding off the empty walls like pattering waves. Eric's skin was warm beneath his hand, warmer than anyone he'd ever felt. Even that soothed him, drawing the ache from his bones that still felt too big for his frame. His darkness rolled under his skin, dripping between them like a fine sieve.

"They'll be back," Eric whispered, his eyes dropping to Zack's lips before flashing back up. "I dragged him — the body — away, but the ones who left? They'll bring more. They won't be looking for me, Zack." Zack reached up and cupped the back of Eric's neck, bringing their foreheads together.

"I'll do the same thing I did to Jared then...or something similar, at least. I never quite know what's going to happen. The lightning was a surprise. It scared the shit out of me, to be honest," said Zack, wrapping his arms around Eric's neck before crawling into the man's lap. His darkness hummed at the contact, sending a shiver up his spine.

Eric had stripped the singed shirt from Zack's body but had left his pants on, probably to maintain his dignity. Now Zack wished that he would have taken everything off when he'd had the chance.

"I've never seen anything like that before — not even from my father. You almost died," said Eric before he let out a long sigh. With Zack on Eric's lap, Eric had to tilt his head and reach up to bring their lips together with the barest of glances. Even the light pressure sent a zing of heat from Zack's lips and straight to his gut. His cock twitched in its confines, longing to press against Eric's strong belly.

"Do you still want to bite me?" Zack asked against Eric's closed lips. As innocent as the kiss was, it still felt absolutely filthy with the tension that was strung between them like LED Christmas lights.

"More than anything."

Chapter Eleven

They moved to the bed in a tangle of limbs and lips. Eric carried him as if he weighed nothing, his lean yet strong frame not even trembling from Zack's weight. Zack wasn't tall or bulky, but he was still a man, and he knew he was too heavy for anyone to be able to lift him so easily. The demon strength that flowed through Eric's veins lit up another set of nerves that Zack didn't even know he had.

There was already a new checklist in his head, this one looking more like a kink checklist than a werewolf one. So far, the top two kinks were raging body heat and super strength. The claw-mark details were a close third. *Who am I kidding?* Eric's gold eyes were definitely at the top.

"Did you run off somewhere?" asked Eric as he pulled back to lick the seam of Zack's lips. "You've got a look on your face like you're thinking really hard."

"Definitely hard," said Zack. "I mean…thinking… thinking really hard…about how sexy you are." He flushed as he stumbled over his words. *Very smooth.*

Eric laughed, the sound so deep and rich that it made Zack flush for a completely different reason. The man was stunning. There was no other word for it. Zack wanted to lick every inch of his body, no matter if he had condoms or not.

"Wait," said Zack, dragging in a deep breath as he was lowered to the bed. Eric paused, his eyes wide and worried.

"You said you couldn't get sick. Is that true for everything?" Zack asked, a smile breaking across his lips as he remembered what Eric had told him. His mind whirled at the possibilities. It was one thing to be immune to the common cold, but another to be immune to everything that could and would come out of a dick.

"My body temperature is eleven degrees warmer than yours. A pathogenic bacteria or virus can't survive or reproduce in my body," said Eric, sounding more like a modern man than an ancient being.

That would explain why he always felt so warm. Even now, with his body hovering over Zack's, heat radiated from him like a furnace.

"So, you can't get STIs or transmit them?" said Zack, crossing his fingers in a hope that his hunch was correct.

"I literally can't transmit anything," Eric deadpanned, leaving no room for argument. His cock was clearly tenting his worn pants, and his impatience was starting to show.

"Fuck, that's so hot," said Zack as he surged up and crashed their lips together. Hot flesh seared against his own, and he opened his mouth, seeking with his tongue as he carded his hands through Eric's long hair. The hair was so soft between his fingers, but it felt thick and wire-like as he gripped it gently to pull Eric closer.

It was so similar to the coyote's fur that he had to wonder just what kind of demon Eric was.

He still didn't get it — the difference between were-animals and demons and what it actually meant about Eric. He wanted him, though — more than he had ever wanted anyone in his life. He wanted to pull him down to the bed and lie back while Eric's searing mouth took him apart. He wanted to repay the favour and see if he could wrap his mouth around Eric's cock.

"I want you to fuck me," said Zack as he pulled back with a gasp. Eric let out a stuttering breath as he widened his gold eyes. His lips were bruised from the fierce kiss, and there was a pink blush across the tanned skin of his nose. Zack could feel Eric's cock through the layers of clothing, and it felt just as big and hard as he remembered.

"We aren't...compatible, Zack. I don't want to hurt you." Eric let out a groan and slid in between Zack's parted thighs. Zack gasped as his cock rubbed against hard flesh when Eric dipped his head down to his neck. Eric's fluttering kisses raised goosebumps, and the scraping of his teeth had Zack biting back another groan.

"What does it mean to you, if you bite me?" Zack panted out between groans. He fisted his hands in Eric's hair, bringing him closer as he begged for more. The thought of a bite was as terrifying as it was exhilarating. A little pain during sex could bring it to a whole new level, but a lot would probably bring his cock crashing down.

"It means that you would be mine," said Eric, his teeth sinking into Zack's flesh hard enough to threaten to bruise. The bruise along the back of Zack's neck throbbed in time with his heart. He couldn't imagine belonging to someone, especially a virtual stranger who lived in the middle of nowhere. Wi-Fi, he could live without. Hydro, running water and a shower curtain...not so much.

He gripped Eric's hair hard and pulled him back up so their lips smashed together. The man tasted like perfection, mixed with a hint of pine that always clung to him. Sometimes the easiest solution was simple avoidance, and that was something Zack excelled at.

"I know I can take you if you just go slow," said Zack as he caught his breath. Their chest's moulded together perfectly. Eric was heavy, but he had to be holding himself up—or maybe he had hollow bones, because Zack could still breathe.

"You can't." Eric shook his head. He pulled back, easing off Zack, but Zack followed with complete determination. He gripped the button of Eric's pants, but he was slapped away like a petulant child. Eric growled, low in his chest, his eyes burning.

Before Zack could protest or try again, he was pushed back to the bed, his head bouncing dangerously close to the wall. His pants were torn from his hips, the button flying away and pinging off the floor. The scraps hung from Eric's clenched fingers, with nothing but ruins remaining.

"You asshole, fuck—"

Eric cut him off by pinning him down with one hand and lowering his mouth over his cock. He took him in one motion, sucking from tip to base with a delicious slurp. His mouth was hot, as if Zack's cock had just dipped into a cup of coffee that was perfect drinking temperature. And the suck was so powerful that Zack's mind blanked.

Who cared that it was his last clean pair of pants, and the only ones that were warm enough for walking around in the snow? Who cared that he was naked while, yet again, Eric was partially clothed with his cock hidden away? And who cared that it was the best blow job he'd ever had?

Zack's heart thudded in his chest as the man sucked him to within an inch of his life, his hips jerking and his toes curling as heat gathered in his groin. His hole clenched around nothing, longing for something inside.

"Put your finger inside me," said Zack, tossing his head back to smack against the pillow. Eric slowed his mouth and lifted off, quirking one eyebrow.

"I don't have any lube."

"You're drooling enough down there to literally sink a ship. It's not my first time, Eric. I can usually take an average cock without much prep. I like a bit of burn anyway. I just need something inside me. Please." Zack rolled his hips, his wet cock wobbling through the air. Drool covered his cock and dripped down to his sac and behind, where his entrance lay. There was probably enough there already that Eric would hardly even have to coat his fingers.

"I've never..." Eric trailed off, looking down at Zack's cock before dipping his gaze lower with a blush flaring across his cheeks. "With demons, we're usually just ready to go. Have to be. Most don't have much control when it comes time to mount."

Mount. That word gave Zack more jitters than *moist.* The word brought violence to mind and pretty much threw consent out of the window. And claiming that they couldn't control themselves, when they were supposed to be some kind of super-powered figment of his imagination?

"Slick up your finger. Stick it in your mouth if there isn't enough there," said Zack, his cock twitching as Eric sucked a finger into his mouth. He watched the line of drool as he pulled it out.

"Drop it down to my sac," he said, waiting until Eric followed his directions before he continued. "Then lower, along the seam. The seam is sensitive there. Go lower, right behind them and push a little... Ungh, that feels good." He took a few deep breaths as Eric unknowingly massaged Zack's prostate from the outside. It already felt amazing, and it would only feel better from the inside.

"Run your finger over my hole. Don't push in yet, just...yeah, that's it. Go around it until you feel me start to relax." *Fuck, it feels so good*. Zack tried to clench to keep the sensations going for longer, but his body was relaxing on its own. "Then push inside, all the way...just go slow. I want to feel you."

The scratch of Eric's nail had Zack's nerves on edge, then he was pushing inside. The intrusion swelled as Eric reached his first knuckle, but it sank in easily, until the entire finger was in. Zack clenched, feeling every inch of it and every groove along the surface. It was so warm and hard.

"Move back and forth a bit and in and out. Go slow, 'cause we don't have lube. If it starts to drag, just add more saliva." Zack shuddered at the obscene sound and feeling of Eric spitting against his slightly stretched hole to slick him up. "Christ, then curl your finger towards my belly. You'll feel something... *Fuck*."

His hips launched off the bed as Eric nailed his prostate dead-on, dragging over the bundle of nerves and making Zack's cock weep. At the same time, Eric was still moving in and out, his finger slick and dragging against Zack in the most wonderful way.

"Put another one in... Fuck, please." He fisted his hands in the sheets as he felt the blunt edge of a second slick finger against his hole. It plunged in, pushing in faster than the first and dragging a yelp from him as it slammed against his prostate.

"Easy," said Zack as he tried to recover an ounce of self-preservation. His cock had dribbled, leaving a pool of pre-cum in his belly button. There was a bit of a burn at his rim, but nothing he couldn't take. His groin was tightening as he got too close for comfort.

"Another," he demanded, needing the burn to push his orgasm back. Eric followed his command, spitting on his rim a second time before easing in a third finger.

It split Zack wide, sending an ache up his spine and giving him something to hold on to that wasn't toe-curling pleasure. Along with the other two, it was already pushing Zack to his limit. Together they were same width as the average cocks he'd taken but nowhere near how big Eric might be.

"Another," said Zack, gripping the sheets and letting out a slow breath to calm himself. He expected Eric to sink in quickly, like he had every time before, but the man stilled instead. Zack blinked in confusion, looking down to where Eric disappeared inside him. He flexed around the intrusion and watched Eric's pupils dilate.

"Another," he said, calmer this time. The zing had faded, and he was truly ready for more this time. He reached out for Eric, smoothing the furrow of concentration on his forehead.

"I'll hurt you," said Eric, shaking his head.

"You won't. I can take more, I promise you. It feels so good, Eric. I want all of you inside me. I want your cock. I want you to mount me...and bite me." The words were out of Zack's mouth before he could stop them. He realised a moment too late that they were absolutely true. He wanted everything from this man.

Eric's eyes dilated until black pushed away the gold rim until it was barely visible. A growl resounded in the cabin, sending a shiver up Zack's spine and making him clench down on Eric's fingers inside him.

Zack let out a sudden breath as Eric lunged at his throat, his teeth pressing into Zack's tender flesh as the same time he withdrew his fingers to Zack's hips. Eric's teeth only left him for a moment as Zack was flipped onto his front with his face pressed into the pillow and his ass in the air and on display. A moment later he was *mounted*.

Eric dug his teeth into the back of his neck, lining up with the same bruises that they had left before. Heat burst against the base of his skull, so much better than the last time, and it pumped his cock full.

Then he felt it. It was slick and so broad that three fingers had been nothing in comparison. It pushed against his hole as Eric ground his hips forwards, trying to push it inside. Zack took a deep breath and let his muscles sag. He'd probably taken bigger toys before, and they had been amazing. The lube issue might cause a problem, but Eric's cock was slicker than anything natural.

With an almighty push, Eric sank inside.

Zack had been very, very wrong. He had never taken anything that big before, not even the toy he had bought as a joke then later tried out. Eric wasn't just big, either. He was hard, unyielding and so hot that he felt like molten steel inside Zack's body. It should have hurt, but it didn't. It was the highest point of pleasure that he'd ever known.

Eric slid inside with a slow steady thrust that had Zack's orgasm threatening like burgeoning storm. Something nudged against Zack's rim—a hand, or something else, Zack wasn't sure—but then Eric was moving and setting a rhythm that had Zack seeing stars.

It was savage and brutal, the pain overwhelming at the same time the pleasure washed over him. Eric was *breeding* him, and Zack fucking loved it.

Three thrusts later, Zack was coming as stars lanced across his vision and set his nerves alight. He clamped down on Eric's cock and Eric bit down, bringing a yelp from deep within Zack's throat. It didn't hurt nearly as much as he had dreaded, but instead only stretched his orgasm longer, until he wondered if it would ever stop coming.

A few more thrusts and Zack felt something molten within him, Eric's hard cock only seeming to swell before it was brutally yanked out of him. A wave of emptiness crashed through his body as Eric pulled back, his teeth leaving a moment after his cock. The sound Zack made was more wounded than when Eric had pushed inside with one long thrust.

Eric's heat returned, his teeth nudging the same spot, but not sinking in this time. He licked over Zack's flesh as he pulled Zack over onto his side, spooning his back against his molten chest that was coated with more than just sweat.

Eric was still hard against his ass, his cock drooling and leaving a cooling line of fluid that dribbled down on the bed. But he was still hard. *How is that even possible?*

Zack rolled his hips, pushing against the hardness that was so rigid that it had to be made of bone. There was no way Eric had gone all the way to his hilt. Zack wasn't even sure it was humanly possible.

Eric grunted before pulling Zack back hard and forcibly stilling his hips. His cock continued to twitch and drool, Eric's hips flexing against Zack's ass as he finally let go of the back of his neck.

"Did you…come?" asked Zack, worried that the man had simply faked it. But there was so much cum — too much to be natural.

"I'm still coming." Eric's voice was thick and strained, his arms tightening around Zack's waist as he continued to twitch. It wasn't like the measly orgasm that Eric had had in the morning. This was something *powerful.*

He growled low and long before his teeth returned. Without the edge of pleasure, the heat of the bite was painful, but not more than Zack could take. Or maybe the lightning had fried some of his nerves back there. It had obviously done wonders for his cock and hole. He'd never been that sensitive before.

"Did you?" asked Eric, his voice still tight.

"Mmm-mm," said Zack. "Best orgasm yet."

Chapter Twelve

"What are you going to do when they come back?" asked Zack, his face tucked against Eric's chest. They had cleaned themselves off then stripped the bed and put on a moderately clean fitted sheet that had been hiding at the bottom of the laundry pile. The blanket was still on the floor by the fire, Zack not needing it any more with Eric's body heat to keep him warm.

"I'm not sure we should be here when they do," said Eric. He curled his hand over Zack's back protectively, holding him close and tight. The scratchy denim that he had donned on the way to fetch a cloth was torture against Zack's over-sensitive member, but he couldn't bring himself to pull away. He could put on pants, but he couldn't even fathom how much effort that would require.

"But they're looking for me, not for you." Zack pushed himself up on his hands, holding himself over Eric. The bruises had faded from Eric's lips and his eyes were half-lidded. His body was more languid than Zack had ever seen it.

Zack was almost ready to flee and leave the snow-ridden hell in the dust, but he had found a little piece of heaven here, too. It was the only reason he hadn't tried to sneak out and trudge his way through the snow, running away to meet another threat head on. He couldn't let Eric turn into another victim of his curse, even if it was indirect.

Eric snorted, turning over to his side and dragging Zack down with him. He nosed at Zack's hair, breathing deep and nuzzling close. "You still smell good, you know. You're bathed in my scent but you're still the best thing I've ever smelled. They would have smelled you, too, and they'll track you wherever you go."

Zack was good at running. He had been running for most of his life. Sure, he had never run from demons before, but he'd already bested them in one fight. How much worse could it get?

"You wouldn't stand a chance," said Eric, seeming to read Zack's thoughts as clearly as his own. "They are more powerful than you could imagine. I am nothing to them...nothing." A frown tugged at his lips as he looked away to the door.

"I seem to recall somebody—not sure who— managed to summon a fucking lightning bolt that blasted one of those demons into smithereens," Zack snarked, pushing himself free and standing from the bed. "I'm best on my own. I always have been. I just need to know how long I have. I don't know if I can get through this snow yet, and it will take a while to clear the roads, especially with the wind picking up again."

Even as he said it, wind buffeted against the cabin and fluttered down the chimney to fan the flames. It had started to snow again as darkness had approached, and although it wasn't blizzard conditions yet, it would be again soon. If they were coming for him now, he would need Eric's help to get back to the road where he could take his chances in the drifts. Any longer, and they might be snowed in for days again.

"They came a long way, I can tell you that," said Eric following every motion as Zack pulled his clothes on. "Jared... He is — was — from a southern legion, but I'm not sure about the other two. If they are moving north and pushing into my father's territory, then they might be closer than I hoped. It will take them weeks to get back to the rest and maybe longer to put together a crew to track you down."

"So long?" said Zack, his heart suddenly calming. He could be halfway across the world in weeks with nothing left but memories of the snow.

"They may be demons, but they were in their human form, so they'll move slower. Technology doesn't... function around us, so even if they shift, they can still only move as fast as their hooves can take them." Eric followed Zack out of the bed and looped his arms around his shoulders. "The snow will hinder them and drain their strength as they run. There is no way the two would stay here alone, not without knowing what you are.

"So, demons can't drive, but they can shift into animals?" Zack shook his head. "I will never fully understand the irony of life. *'I can't get the car started, so how about we just run for thirteen days?'*" That amount of exercise would probably kill him. No, not probably... definitely.

"Some have hooves and others have paws. It depends on the bloodlines, just like were-animals. Some spend their entire lives trapped and end up at the wrong end of a hunter's gun." He touched Zack's chin, bending down for a brief kiss before he wandered to the kitchen, filling the kettle from the barrel.

"So, I assume you have paws," said Zack, watching as Eric nodded from the kitchen. He wondered what Eric would look like, and if he would be small and sleek like his brother, or bigger like the ancient wolf he'd said his father was. "What was Jared?" Maybe it was because he was dead, but his fear had drained away to nothing. A dead man couldn't hurt him.

"He was a horse—and a big one, too. He looked something like an old-style draft when he shifted." Eric placed the kettle within the flames, his hand lingering in the fire for longer than was strictly necessary. The flames seemed to dance around him, as if his arm were just another part of them.

"Holy shit, he did have a horse-cock. I knew it." Zack laughed as Eric scrunched his nose up in distaste. "All I could think about was my grandfather's stallions when I saw that hunk of meat swaying in the wind. How could a guy even do anything with something like that? He would have to be a two-pump chump or he'd just pass out with all that blood going from his tiny little brain."

Eric chuckled, shaking his head and grabbing the poker to stoke the coals. They flared to life as another gust of wind fluttered down the chimney. "I can confirm that he was a two-pump chump. One actually, on his first try. And it took him an entire day to get it back up again."

Zack felt the blood drain from his face. How had he forgotten? Jared had leered at Eric, illuding to the fact that they had had a relationship. It hadn't sounded exactly consensual.

"Was it... I mean...did he?" Zack couldn't say the words. If he did, he would have to find a way to bring Jared back to life, just so he could fry him all over again.

"I wanted it, if that's what you're asking," said Eric, his voice calm and low. "I was lonely, and he was the only compatible demon close by. It was years ago, anyway, and the edge of that poor decision dulled a while ago." Eric leaned forwards, his voice dropping. "To be honest, it was the biggest cock I'd ever seen, and I wanted to try something new and interesting."

"Oh my God," Zack squealed, moving in front of the fire so he could be closer to Eric. "You blush and stammer in the bedroom like some kind of virgin, but you're actually a size queen."

"I don't think I'm the only size queen." Eric laughed as Zack pouted, grabbing the blanket and draping it over his shoulders. "I'm glad you're a size queen, Zack. It means that you might be able to keep up with me." His eyes dilated in the low light as the night sank its claws into the dwindling sunlight.

Zack peeked down at Eric's groin, letting out a small gasp as he saw what was waiting for him there. His mouth watered at the idea of taking Eric into his mouth and sucking him down as far as he could, which would only be a few inches. His ass was still sore from the stretch and there was a slight burn from the lack of lube, but his mouth was fine.

Zack did his best impression of a lunge, which was more like a graceless fall, into Eric's lap, grabbing the button on his jeans and attempting to pry it open. Attempting, because Eric gripped his hands, stilling them and his efforts with a deep frown.

"You have to be kidding me," said Zack, looking up at Eric through his light lashes. "You have literally been balls deep in my ass. You aren't allowed to be shy anymore. I want to see your cock. The suspense might kill me if I don't."

"I wasn't balls deep," said Eric, his voice low and quiet. His pupils had narrowed, all signs of arousal gone except for the tent in his pants. "Trust me... You would know if I was. What you got was a solid sixty percent. Besides, I have to make dinner and it's too late for something frozen from the cold storage. I'll have to go get something fresh." He moved Zack's hands away from him and stood from the floor gracefully.

Zack spluttered, falling to his elbows from the shock of yet another rejection. Who the hell turned down a blow job? Eric must've been on the verge of starvation. And sixty percent? Zack's ass throbbed in protest. He was never going to survive this man.

Zack's stomach growled as Eric reached the door, forgoing his coat again and stripping out of his shirt. His pants slithered to the floor, leaving a perfect view of his tanned ass. No tan lines, with each cheek the same shade as the skin on his arms. His ass was round and high and the perfect size for squeezing, and Zack had the sudden urge to bite it.

Eric opened the door, tossing a smile over his shoulder before he disappeared through the crack. A gust of cold fluffed the room, stealing the heat from Zack's skin, but Eric hadn't looked cold in the least— not even one goosebump on his perfect skin.

The hair on his arms stood straight up as Zack heard *something* over the steady battering of the wind. It was a mix between a crack, a squelch and a sound that reminded him of someone rolling into a ditch, vomiting, then breaking their arm.

He scrambled to the door, pulling it wide and looking out into the swirling snow, just in time to see something disappear into the forest. It was huge, like the shadow of bear that moved with the speed of an eagle. He blinked the snow from his eyes, trying to get a bettering look at the shape.

A fluffy dark tail disappeared through the trees.

Chapter Thirteen

Zack had expected a rabbit, or maybe a bird, or something that could be carried by a normal person, when Eric had decided to look for *fresh* meat. He watched the edge of the tree line from the door, waiting for the dark shadow to appear so he could get a look at Eric's shifted body. It was more exciting than opening a Christmas present.

Instead, he saw the tawny fur of the coyote appear at the edge of the forest. His heart thudded as it approached the cabin. It was walking with only a slight limp, its lean body steady and matted fur coated with snow. It made its way slowly to the porch, looking back over its shoulder as it reached the step.

Before it could get any closer, something appeared that looked more like a figment of Zack's imagination than anything that could be real. It was dark black with streaks of gold and red along its hackles and flanks. The fluffy black tail alone was nearly as large as the coyote, although its snout was snubbed, and almost feline in appearance. Large paws skimmed over the snow without sinking more than an inch, even with the deer hanging from its massive jaws.

Gold eyes snapped to Zack's as the creature dropped the deer from its mouth and licked the blood from its jowls. The coyote turned, rushing forwards with its head and tail low. When he moved to bite the fallen deer, the larger creature snapped its teeth, snarling until the coyote backed off. The sound opened a pit of absolute terror beneath Zack's feet.

It was a wolf, but unlike anything Zack had ever seen. He wasn't sure if there was any human alive out there that had seen it, either. It was nearly the size of a pony, for Christ's sakes.

Light suddenly shimmered within the dark snow, the sun nearly gone from the clouded sky. The same gagging sound that Zack had heard before followed, then a crack that was loud enough to be heard for a mile, before the wolf simply disappeared. There was no morphing or falling hair as it turned back into Eric. It simply disappeared, leaving Eric standing before the downed deer with a streak of fresh blood down his chest.

Eric dragged the deer to the cabin, the view of his naked body blocked by the tawny fur. He retrieved something from the porch before he tied a rope and slung it over the roof support. The deer swayed in the breeze as it was hung, its limbs loose like the freshly dead.

Zack looked away, stepping back as the scent of copper hit him. His time in the doorway, although brief, had drained the warmth from his limbs, leaving him stiff and tired. His stomach flopped as he thought of the deer with its eyes cloudy and sightless.

It was one thing to eat meat, but it was something completely different to watch a naked demon drag a deer from the forest and hang it on the porch.

Eric stepped through the door, facing away and grabbing his clothes and jacket before stepping back outside. Zack let out a sigh and slumped to the floor. Never in all his life had he met someone so shy and awkward about their cock. Sure, it felt bigger than average, but it couldn't be as bad as Eric thought it was.

Maybe it was covered in giant moles? Which was an image that was too disturbing to give much merit. It could have been like that broken cock that Zack had once seen in a documentary, that looked like it had an elbow. But it had been inside him, and it definitely felt straight... or not. He racked his brain, thinking of other possibilities but came up blank.

A dick was a dick. They weren't always the prettiest things in the world, but Zack liked them. Even the ones that were under average were still nice to look at. And the big ones? Well, they were like a cherry on chocolate ice cream.

Guys usually couldn't wait to show him their dicks or thrust them into his mouth when he offered and dropped to his knees. But Eric had been alone for so long, and his past experiences didn't exactly sound stellar. Maybe he just didn't know what to do when someone was offering — or maybe he was just self-conscious. Lovers like Jared could do that to a person and make them feel ugly, even if they were attractive.

And Eric *was* attractive. He was the elusive ten that only popped up in movies or magazines that had been digitally edited for hours. Who needed Hollywood when the forest was hiding the good ones?

Zack watched Eric closely as the man returned with a literal piece of leg that had been stripped of its fur. He moved smoothly with his legs set just apart, like any man with a normal package would walk. When he bent over to put the meat on the rack in the fireplace, his legs were splayed to give his dick space. Zack could scarcely see the outline of it, now soft in his pants. He should've made an effort to look closer when the man had been hard.

"Hopefully I got it back fast enough," said Eric as he backed away from the flames and licked the blood from his fingers. Zack shuddered and suppressed a gag, changing his mind about going in for a kiss. Eric would have to brush his teeth first…and gargle.

"You were gone for less than ten minutes," said Zack. "If it were me, I would still be out there. Hell, I would be out there all night with nothing to show for it but a few pine needles and some bark." Maybe not even the bark, if he couldn't get it off the tree. Nature was tough.

"Pine needles can treat vitamin C deficiency, so you'd be good on that front. But with meat, if the animal goes into rigor, then you have to let it rest for a few days before it's edible again. If you get it in the fire fast enough, it doesn't get quite so tough. It will still be chewy, though, so your jaw might ache a bit." Eric stoked the flames with the poker before he wandered to the kitchen, returning with a glass of pre-boiled water for each of them.

"I don't mind a sore jaw," said Zack, quirking one brow. "I actually kind of like it." He set his water to the side and waited for Eric to do the same before he pounced…tooth brushing forgotten.

Most men would have made an *oompf* noise if a full-grown man leapt into their lap, but not Eric. He tensed his thighs as Zack landed and caught him by the hips to lower him down gently. He took Zack's weight as if it were nothing, his arms hardly straining.

"Well, hello there," said Eric, his gold eyes level with Zack's. Zack's gaze flickered down to Eric's lips that were still stained bright with a smudge of blood. Was it terrible that it made the man even more attractive than he already was? It must've been Zack's inner caveman that made his cock stand to attention. Eric was already matching him, his cock hard against Zack's ass.

"I want you to know that this is a judgement-free zone," said Zack, looping his arms around Eric's neck so the man hopefully wouldn't try to escape. "So, I'm going to tell you an embarrassing story, and you aren't going to laugh. Then you are going to tell me what's up, and I won't laugh, either." He ground down as Eric furrowed his forehead with concern and tightened his grip on Zack's hips.

"This isn't about being embarrassed. This is about trust." Zack leaned in so their foreheads touched, taking a deep breath. *Pine and woodsmoke, with something dark and dangerous.* His inner-caveman roared, bringing him to full mast.

"I trust you, Eric." He took a deep breath and let his eyes fall shut. He hadn't said that before, because it hadn't been true. Something had changed within him in the last day, and he found himself actually trusting someone for the first time in his life. "The first time I topped someone, I came before I got the condom all the way on." There it was. The most embarrassing moment of his life. It would have been okay if he had been young and innocent, but no. He had been twenty-five the first time he'd decided to stray from bottoming. Twenty-five and he'd still come in his hand.

Eric roared with laughter, tilting his head back and the sound erupting from deep within his chest. Zack smacked him before leaning back and crossing his arms. He couldn't stop the pout or the slight feeling of betrayal.

"I said no laughing."

"How could I not?" asked Eric before he wiped his watering eyes with the back of his hand. "I mean, how did that even work? Did you still try to put your soft cock inside him and squish it around?" He let out another laugh, his eyes crinkling at the corners. "Did he even feel it?" Eric snorted…actually fucking snorted.

"No," Zack sighed and let his shoulders droop while he stared at the worn wooden flooring. "I just… You know how your cock still stays hard for a bit after you come? Well, I got the condom on the rest of the way and just rammed it inside him before I got soft. I didn't want him to realise that I'd already come, so I just went as fast as I could, trying to stay hard."

"And?"

"He pushed me away and said I was being too rough for him." And that was the second most embarrassing moment for Zack—the moment when he'd tried to avoid embarrassment by accidentally hurting someone.

"I hope he was okay in the end," said Eric, his humour dropping away.

Zack shrugged. "Yeah, he was fine. I felt terrible about it, though." He was lucky that his curse hadn't reared up and snapped at the man for pushing him away. He peered back up through his blond lashes, catching Eric's gaze and holding it. "Now will you tell me?"

"Tell you what?" Eric rolled his hips once, bringing his cock up against the seam of Zack's ass. Zack could've sworn that he was still a little bit open. It would be so easy to get prepped this time around.

"Why can't I see your dick?" He lifted up on his knees and peered down at the tent beneath him. He could see the outline — thick, long and straining beneath the fabric. It looked so good.

"I...just... We aren't compatible," said Eric, a flush blooming across his cheeks. From this close, Zack could see a tiny smattering of freckles on Eric's otherwise-flawless skin. It made him look more human and less like the demon that Zack knew him to be.

"See? You've said that before, but I really liked your dick. I think it fit perfectly and I would love to do that again...frequently." He reached down and ran his hand over the fabric. Eric's cock twitched beneath his palm, the heat of him radiating.

"It's because of who I am — what I am. It's not like yours, exactly," said Eric, tripping over his words as his blush spread down his neck. His gaze dropped and his hands trembled on Zack's hips.

"If you are trying to make me less curious, you are failing miserably." His stomach clenched as he ground down on Eric's hot cock that was so impossibly hard. "Fuck, please let me see you. I just want to taste you on my tongue and feel you in my mouth. I hope I can fit it in my mouth, because I want that more than anything." Zack pulled his last trump card out of his hat — dirty talk. He wasn't that great at it, but if it didn't convince Eric, then nothing would.

Gold eyes flashed and suddenly they were moving. Eric carried them to the bed and tossed Zack down onto the blanket. Zack bounced once before he shimmied up on his elbows, glaring at the man who'd tossed him like he was a little kid. Sure, it was hot sometimes, but it was also a bit emasculating.

The glare fell off his face when Eric dropped his hands to the waistband of his pants, toying with the button as he chewed his lip. He slipped his eyes shut, and in one motion, he tugged the waistband down, leaving him completely bare.

A dark trail of trimmed hair was the first thing that Zack saw before Eric's cock was revealed — and what a cock it was. It was jutting out completely perpendicular to his body and was flushed pink, nearly red. It was long but also thick, which Zack already knew intimately. It looked like a cock. It was bigger than average, and uncut, but still a cock.

He crawled until he could feel the heat of it against his lips, taking a deep breath of Eric's strong scent. It made his head swim and heat flare at the base of his spine, reminding him that he was empty.

Upon closer inspection, he could see blond and red streaking through the trimmed curls and noticed that the pinkish tinge of Eric's cock was a slightly different from his own. He still didn't get what Eric was trying to hide, but he wasn't one to turn down a challenge.

He slid his fingers over the half-hidden mushroom-shaped head, relishing as Eric's body twitched and his gold eyes snapped open. The surface was slick, much slicker than it should be, as if it had its own personal lubricant. *Convenient, but not off-putting.* The shaft was slippery and smooth but rock hard beneath Zack's hand, as if there were a bone beneath his palm.

"It's so hard," said Zack, moving so his lips hovered closer to the tip. His mouth watered as he took another deep breath. Eric smelled so good.

There was a drop of pearly fluid at the tip of his cock, and the rest of it was shiny, as if there were a layer of oil that had already been rubbed on it.

"I like this," said Zack as he ran his hand down the shaft again just to feel how slick it was. "Is it like this all the time?" He brought a finger to his mouth to taste the slickness. It was warm and heady with just a touch a salt.

"Just before...um," said Eric, his mouth falling open as Zack leaned in and licked the pre-cum from the tip. It was much stronger, with a hint of sweetness. It certainly wouldn't make a good cocktail, but it was good as far as cum went.

Zack gripped the base, squeezing just enough to feel the throb beneath his palm. He sank his fingers into flesh that was so much softer than the rest of the shaft. He moved closer, pressing down again and watching his fingers sink into the lax surface. Eric's breath stuttered, and he threaded his hand into Zack's hair.

Encouraged by Eric's reaction, he opened his mouth wide and sucked the tip into his mouth, careful to keep his teeth well back. He flexed his hand, loving the way that Eric's breath hitched as he lowered his mouth, swirling his tongue around and around.

He stopped at three inches, his lips stretched so wide that his jaw was aching already.

Eric groaned low enough that it was almost a growl, and the flesh in Zack hand *swelled*. Zack pulled back, squeezing again as he tried to understand what he was feeling. It *had* grown at the base, now more than one-and-a-half times thicker than the rest of the shaft and was growing still.

"It's a knot," said Eric as he took a deep breath, his whole body tense. "It ties me to my partner to make sure I can't pull out during breeding." His eyes fluttered closed again as Zack moved his hand away.

"It's really sensitive," said Zack, trying to understand. "I don't remember…that." He would have known if that had been inside him, locking them together while Eric filled him.

Fuck, that sounded amazing. Zack shuddered, his hole clenching on nothing.

"I didn't put it inside you. I think it would hurt you—a lot. It gets big…really big." Even with Zack's hand gone, the flesh had still continued to swell, the rest of the shaft turning bright red.

"Well, this definitely wasn't what I was expecting, but it's actually really hot." He touched the knot again, holding the burning flesh in his hand and squeezing. He didn't even get his mouth back onto Eric's cock before white fluid leapt from the tip, spraying his face and chest.

Eric groaned, his hold going tight in Zack's hair and his hips jerking. His knot got bigger under Zack's hand, pushing his fingers farther and farther apart. Then it got even bigger. His mouth hung open in shock when it finally stopped growing, cum leaking from Eric's tip in a quiet stream.

"Oh," Eric groaned, his head thrown back in obvious utter ecstasy and his hands tight.

Zack leaned in, taking the tip into his mouth again before he sucked. Flavour burst over his tongue in a bouquet that was familiar and yet unique. He swallowed, but it kept coming.

"How much do you have in there?" asked Zack, his eyes going wide. Eric was *still* coming. It had slowed to a dribble, but his hips were shaking and his sac was drawn up tight as his orgasm continued.

Oh, the envy. Zack was lucky to get five seconds out of his orgasm from start to finish, longer if he edged the fuck out of himself. But it had been a minute, and Eric was still twitching. He had seemed to last forever when they had been spooned together, too.

"No one's ever done that," said Eric, his voice tight and strained as he continued to groan. "But when my knot is inside someone, with them squeezing me tight, sometimes it can be an hour before it stops."

An hour-long orgasm? Was there a sign-up sheet somewhere that Zack could put his name on?

"What would happen if I let go now?" asked Zack, easing the pressure just a bit. The knot was firm, but not nearly as hard as the rest of the red shaft. Eric hissed as Zack's hand moved, placing his own hand over Zack's and squeezing it tight again.

"It's like the worst case of blue-balls you've ever had, mixed with someone pinching the end of your dick when you're trying to come. It hurts — and not in a good way." Eric caught his gaze, his body losing every bit of tension that he'd been carrying. His grip went soft, carding through Zack's hair and spreading bits of slick through the strands.

"I should be okay now," said Eric with his eyes clear.

Zack eased off slowly, watching for any sign of discomfort before he dropped his hand. He was liberally coated in fluids that were rapidly drying all over his skin. It wasn't quite as sticky as his own cum would have been, but it was still gross as it started to dry.

"I can warm up some water for you if you want another shower," said Eric, still running his hand through Zack's hair. "I could join you if you like. And return the favour." His gaze dropped to Zack's lap, where his cock perked up as if it had just heard its name.

"I would like that."

After a jaw-aching meal of tough and tasteless venison, the night devolved into steamy kisses and slow sucks as Eric took Zack into his mouth and water slowly cascaded down their bodies from the filled watering can. Zack came embarrassingly quickly from Eric's mouth alone before he dragged Eric back to the bed, bringing their lips together before twining their limbs and resting his head on Eric's chest. His heart was a slow and steady beat that drew him down into the depths of a dreamless sleep.

Chapter Fourteen

"Is there ever a cell phone signal out here?" asked Zack as he moved up onto the bed, standing on the mattress and reaching for the ceiling with one arm. The more hours that passed in the cabin, the more he longed for a glimpse of the outside world that wasn't snow-covered.

In his hand was his cell phone that had finally decided to turn on. The battery was redlined, and the screen flickered every time he turned it a certain way, but it was still kind of working. The signal was a dead-zero, and no matter where he paced, it stayed that way.

"This whole area is in my father's territory, and no one lives here except for a few like myself," said Eric from the kitchen where he was bent over a sink full of dishes. "Demons and technology don't get along very well." He walked over to Zack before placing one finger on the screen.

It went utterly blank, as if the battery had been plucked from the case. Zack shook it, slamming the power button in frustration. As soon as Eric moved away again, it fluttered back to life.

"It's why we tend to avoid big cities and why we can't drive or fly anywhere." Back in the kitchen, he plunged his hands back into the suds and scraped a bit of gristle off a small white plate.

"Ug, this is so frustrating. I think I'll go try outside." Zack hopped off the bed when he saw Eric shrug before continuing to scrub. Eric was shirtless and utterly delicious as suds crept their way up to his elbows, but Zack's cock was too tired for another round so soon. He'd lost count of his orgasms, and they'd run out of clean sheets, too.

He bundled in as many layers as he could, pulling two pairs of socks on and Eric's furred jacket, before he stepped outside.

The storm had finally ceased, but the temperature had dropped to the point where his nostrils froze as soon as he stepped out of the door. In his regular jacket, he would have been frozen in a few minutes, but Eric's gear was surprisingly efficient. Zack hadn't been brave enough to ask him what animal the fur had come from, but he was pretty sure he'd eaten a part of it. Eric seemed to love to feed him little bits of everything from cold storage or whatever he caught in the forest.

The drifted snow was piled against the front door, but there was a small path from Eric coming and going as he'd retrieved more wood. Luckily, he had also removed the deer carcass after slicing roasts and storing them in cold storage. The blood had been covered by fresh snow, and the smell had blown away on the wind.

Zack took a deep breath, scrunching his nose as it tingled, and stepped out to his car. It was half-buried, and he dreaded the moment when he would have to shovel his way out of the lane and back to the main road. He still didn't know how Eric had even got it back this far in the first place.

Something in his chest tightened as he thought about leaving. As desolate as this place was, it had grown on him over the last few days. He'd got used to the inconsistent temperature of the cabin, and the constant need to pile wood on the fire. He'd even got used to showering out of a watering can.

The air was crisp, and it was so quiet that it made his ears ring—no cars, no voices, no hum of electricity…only the wind and one blue jay that was starting to drive him mad.

But he couldn't stay. He couldn't risk Eric's life by sticking around when the legion of demons returned for him—and they would come. Eric had assured him of that several times. Eric had also tried to convince him that the cabin was the safest place for him, as they were on his father's territory. There was nowhere they could run where they wouldn't be found.

He still remembered how the coyote had crumpled as it had been tossed into a tree—how its teeth hadn't made a dent on the demon's flesh, even though it had lunged for the kill, and how Eric had screamed and begged them to stop. His father hadn't come to their rescue then.

That couldn't happen again. *I have to move on.*

His cell phone pinged repeatedly in his hand as he found a sliver of service, and every text message he'd missed came in at once. There were eleven messages, all from the same number—one that he didn't recognise. His blood ran cold as he opened the first one.

It was from his ex's brother, a man he hadn't even met. There hadn't been any reason for them to really meet, either. They hadn't been together that long, and their relationship was barely skin deep.

The words blurred in front of his eyes as he scrolled through the notifications. His ex was...dead.

He stared at the phone as blood rushed through his ears, cutting off the calls of the single jay. He couldn't breathe, even though his lungs ached for nourishment.

His body was frozen, but he couldn't stop himself from reading the messages on the dull screen. The first asked him where he was and what had happened. The second was the same, and the third. From there, queries morphed into accusations and threats. The last was confirmation that the police had been informed and would be looking for him. It didn't so much ask him to turn himself in than demand it.

He thought it would have been fine. The moment his ex had snarled at him when he had accidentally dropped a glass mug, Zack had gone straight for his go-bag and boots. The shouting hadn't stopped until his voice dropped to a plea as Zack hastily packed. Zack hadn't responded, knowing that there just wasn't time. He'd had to get out of there before something bad happened.

When he'd stepped out of the apartment and into the chilly hallway, the guy had been alive, even if he had been sobbing on the other side of the door. Zack had run down the steps, nearly tripping on the last one, before he'd darted for his car. He'd been driving before his seatbelt was clipped. He hadn't looked in the rear-view mirror. He'd just run.

The guy had been nice—forgettable, but nice. He had a sweetness that most people grew out of when they hit their thirties and started to see the bitterness in the world. That had been why Zack had taken the risk and agreed to stay after a one-night fling. His ex had needed someone to live with, and Zack had needed somewhere to stay. It had been perfect until Zack had reached for a photo mug in the cupboard and it had slipped from his fingers.

Now the guy was dead...over a fucking mug. And Zack hadn't even known. He was in the middle of nowhere getting his rocks off while his ex's family was demanding answers and trying to plan a funeral.

They would never find him there, but he couldn't stay forever. Eric seemed to be immune to his curse — or maybe he just hadn't triggered anything yet — but the demons were coming for Zack. And Zack knew in his heart that they wouldn't be coming to ask questions.

Revenge sounded very demon-like.

Zack heard the crunch in the snow a moment before his phone's screen flashed the battery symbol and went blank. He shoved it into the pocket of his pants, leaving his hands there to warm under the layers. The cold suddenly seeped in, and he realised that he had been standing there long enough for his feet to go numb. The tears on his face had frozen against his cheeks, leaving him even colder.

He looked up, expecting Eric to be there, looking at him with concern. He saw a pair of hungry yellow eyes and tawny fur. There was still blood matted to the coyote's jaws, as if they had never been clean.

Terror bloomed in his gut.

The coyote was less than two steps away from him, and close enough that one leap would close the space between them. Its hackles were up, and his head was high as he scented the air. Its grey tail swung lazily back and forth in either uncertainty or aggression.

It took another step, its paw sinking in the snow and crunching against the frozen surface. Zack moved back, starting when he slammed into his car door. He had nowhere to go, and the coyote was still advancing, its black nose a few scant centimetres away.

It sniffed the fur jacket that Zack had donned, sneezing once before licking its lips. Zack's heart thudded in his chest as he caught sight of the large canines in the coyote's mouth. They looked so sharp and pearly white, even against the snow.

Zack gasped as it turned and suddenly rubbed its great head right along Zack's stomach, in the same way a cat would scent his hand. Only this creature had to weigh one-hundred pounds, and it was putting every bit of that behind the nudge of its head.

He braced himself against the car as the coyote moved its head back and forth, scenting Zack and pushing against his vulnerable belly. With each great swipe, it moved a bit closer, until there was no room between them at all. Zack panted, gripping the frozen frame of his car.

"Please don't eat me," said Zack, his voice nothing more than a whisper. His body shook as the coyote cocked his head and lifted itself onto his hind paws, tossing its front paws over Zack's shoulders. It was tall enough that they stood eye to eye, and its mouth was at the perfect height to bite his neck. He could feel the warmth of its breath against him, and he could smell the copper tinge.

This thing had tried to kill him before, and it had tried to kill a demon, too. Its crumpled body was completely healed and looked no worse for wear. It wasn't even limping, and its eyes were bright and lucid.

Zack's breath stuttered to a halt as it nuzzled his neck, the cold tinge of its nose freezing him to his core. It was the same thing that Eric had done — repeatedly — but this felt so much further on the wrong side of danger. This was a man trapped in the body of a wild beast, one that was unstable and possibly a little insane — one that had been trapped longer than Zack had been alive.

Its rough tongue swiped at his neck and something in Zack broke. He had finally had enough of not having control of his life. Nothing was going to take his life away from him again, or anyone else's without his consent. He was done.

"Get off *now*," said Zack, dropping his voice into a growl the way Eric had done. It sounded ridiculous coming out of his mouth and more like a puppy than the wolf he was trying to imitate. The coyote didn't even pause, its great tongue slobbering every inch of his exposed neck.

Zack tried to reach for the darkness that was usually right under the layer of his skin, but the thrum was out of his reach. It was deep in his bones, keeping him warm against the chill of the air, but it refused to budge.

"I said *off.*" Zack slammed his knee up, putting every bit of his strength behind it. He had one chance to make an impression and get this *thing* to back off. If he broke a rib, hopefully it would heal...after Zack had slipped away from it, of course.

The blow had the opposite effect that Zack had been hoping for. The coyote twisted, dancing on its hind legs as it took the blow, absorbing it with zero effort as if Zack were nothing more than a pesky fly. Its teeth, which had been covered by its lips thus far, shot out and sank into Zack's shoulder.

The fur coat caught most of the blow as the coyote snarled quietly in his ear, jerking back and forth until Zack fell off balance and crashed down into the snow. The grip never left his shoulder, pushing hard enough to bruise through the layers.

He tried to scream for Eric, but the fall had pushed the air from his lungs. He scrambled on the ground, hardly able to breathe as the weight of the were-coyote hit him.

The coyote growled as it jerked from side to side, tearing the furs from him in a frenzy. His coat went next, with much less resistance, and part of his shirt followed. His spine brushed against freezing snow, stealing the heat from his body.

He was naked from sternum to shoulder as the coyote lunged back in, his teeth sinking into Zack's flesh as if he were bubble wrap just waiting to be popped.

He screamed.

Chapter Fifteen

The teeth slipped through his skin as if he were made of nothing more than paper, and at first, it didn't even hurt. There was a sudden rush of warmth that moved from his shoulder and down to his chest as if he'd just stepped into a hot shower. Then there was an ache, like nothing more than a pulled muscle from vigorous sex after three days of sitting on a couch.

Only then did the pain set in. It was a blistering heat that pushed a scream from deep within his lungs, loud enough that somewhere an avalanche was just getting started.

The coyote went still, its hot breath sweeping over Zack's shoulder as he tightened his grip. Zack writhed, doing everything he could to break free from the hold. He smashed his fists against the canine's face and tore at its mouth with his nails, but nothing seemed to faze it. The movement tugged at the connection, lighting up every nerve in the most terrible way.

Then, something settled.

His darkness reached for the coyote, in the same way that it had reached for Eric. It drained the energy from his body, as if he were a leaky faucet that had been left to drip for too long.

Zack slumped down into the snow as lethargy consumed him. His lashes fluttered against the sunlight as he gazed up into the grey sky where tiny snowflakes were slowly circling down. It was so bright, and his shoulder felt so warm, even with the snow beneath him. One hand clutched chilled, thick fur that was so much softer than he remembered, and the other fisted the snow as it melted in his palm.

A thundering growl pulled him from his haze, his eyes snapping wide as the teeth moved in his flesh, pushing deeper. The growl didn't come from the coyote, but the massive dark creature that lumbered towards them through the deep snow. The lips of its short snout were pulled back in a snarl, showing off pearly white teeth that were so much larger than the ones inside him.

It took him three full seconds before he realised what he was looking at — *who* he was looking at. The tattered scraps of shorts were the first clue to the identity of the beast — and the familiar dark coat with streaks of red and blonde. The gold eyes were familiar, but they had lost their civility, leaving something wild behind.

"Eric," said Zack, his voice weaker than he'd expected. He tried to swallow the lump in his throat, but he was just too tired. His hand flopped down, leaving the fur of the coyote and thudding into the snow.

Eric stopped a few paces away, his head low and his tail erect over his back. Another grumble shook Zack to his core and made every hair on his body stand. He was massive, nearly the height of Zack's chest if he hadn't been pinned to the snow. He was longer than his car was wide, not including his bushy tail.

The coyote quivered and let out a low whine that vibrated Zack's skin, but he didn't release his hold. Even as Eric stepped closer, his snarling mouth hovering over the vulnerable neck of his brother, the coyote still didn't loosen its grasp.

Eric snapped his jaws next to his brother's face and the coyote finally let go, but it didn't flee. It turned to Eric, going straight for his neck. Eric shot out one paw, missing the coyote by centimetres as it ducked and flung itself to the side. When their bodies finally met, it was like watching two wild animals fence—and they were fighting to the death.

Clumps of fur landed in the snow, only to be blown away on the breeze. A splash of blood followed a deep yelp as the coyote managed to capture Eric's paw in its mouth. Gold eyes hardened, and the coyote never had the advantage again.

The coyote was suddenly pinned, bleeding and yelping while Eric loomed over him with his throat in his grasp. Blood poured from the half-demon, hidden in his dark fur, but not in the snow beneath. Other than a few clumps of missing hair, the coyote appeared to be mostly unharmed.

Zack tried to move, but an ache lanced up his shoulder that sent him back down into the snow. It burned, more than any paper cut or broken bone he'd ever had. It felt like he imagined pepper spray would feel on top of vinegar in an open wound.

Rabies was his first thought. He was going to die of rabies, and he couldn't even go to a hospital because the cops were looking for him. And if he didn't die of rabies within the next five seconds, then he was going to become a were-coyote. Someone bitten by a werewolf always turned. Everyone knew that.

Either way, his little curse was about to be the least of his problems.

"Zack! Zack, are you with me?" Eric's face appeared above him in a way that seemed so reminiscent. It was like he'd been struck by lightning again, only this time, he didn't think Eric could save him from the wound.

"I don't want to be a werewolf," said Zack, hoping he had said it and not just thought it. Eric didn't answer, instead just lifted him from the ground and carried him until the sky disappeared and a familiar wooden ceiling appeared. "I feel like living out here is a huge hazard. You need to put up signs—like 'wet floor' signs, only more…lethal," Zack mumbled. Since he'd arrived in this general area of the world, everything in his life had literally gone wrong—except one thing, of course…Eric.

"You are a walking hazard," said Eric so low that Zack wasn't sure if he was actually supposed to hear the words. "Ten minutes. You're outside for ten minutes, and you manage to get mauled and claimed by my brother. If you hadn't screamed…" His voice trailed off as Zack's back hit the bed.

"Am I going to turn?" Zack asked. He knew so little of Eric's world, but he still insisted on fucking the guy. Hell, if his shoulder didn't hurt so much and his head wasn't swimming, he would've offered to blow the guy right then as a thank you. He wanted to get his hands back on that knot.

"Were-animals are born, not turned—not like in the books. He wasn't trying to harm you, Zack. He was claiming you. The bleeding's stopped, but the bite is big. He doesn't have control of himself."

Zack felt Eric's warm hand shift across his throat before he touched the wound. The heat from the touch was so soothing that he relaxed, melting into the bed and letting out a sigh.

"Claim… Is that a sex thing, like when you said it?" He tried to focus on the ceiling — or Eric's face or anything except the swimming in his head, but he was floating, his voice echoing as he spoke.

"Yes." Eric's voice was tight.

"He's practically a dog. Maybe you forgot to explain the birds and the bees to him, but that's not going to work." Zack laughed and shook his head, the movement enraging the ache in his shoulder.

"He doesn't know that. A part of him is there, and that part of him that isn't trapped was telling him to claim you. Lie still. The bite is almost healed." Eric's grip was firm, searing Zack's skin. A moan caught, low in his throat.

"What? How?" Zack tried to sit up to get a look in a mirror, before he remembered that there wasn't one. He'd shaved with a straight razor in the reflection of the window because Eric had declared that he had no reason to look at himself every day. If Zack looked like that, he would never step away from the mirror.

"Our saliva has healing properties. Most things that aren't human do. The bite I gave you healed instantly, before you could even bleed. A bite from a were-animal takes a bit longer, and it hurts a hell of a lot more."

"It burns," said Zack as he tried to claw at Eric's hand. The burning wasn't getting any better. If anything, it was getting worse. His sight cleared, and Eric snapped into focus. The man was bleeding from the arm that was touching Zack, the jagged wound raw and ragged.

"I know." Eric hissed through his teeth as his arm flexed. A fresh wave of blood seeped from the wound and dripped down his arm. Zack gagged.

"It would have burned when I bit you, too, but you accepted me — welcomed me — asked for it. Anything else will just hurt you." His blood trickled onto Zack's chest where his coat was still barely clinging. The furs were gone, lost in the snow.

"That seems a little unfair, that the victim is the one that feels the fallout of an unwelcomed bite," said Zack, the burning finally starting to ease to a morbid itch. It reminded him of the cold that had seeped into his bones when the other demons had threatened them. It was such a feeling of wrongness.

"Don't worry. He felt it, too, but in his mouth and on his face." Eric leaned back and released Zack's wound, clutching his dripping one instead. "That's probably why he wasn't letting go. He was waiting for you to submit and accept it, but he was just making it worse. We can't touch anything without consent." The skin on his arm was smudged red, with nothing but a shrinking pink line where the bite had been.

"You'll scar. You don't heal like a demon." Eric shrugged, looking down at himself and flushing. Zack followed the gaze, realising that Eric was utterly naked. The remnants of his pants that had clung to his hips when he had shifted, had been lost somewhere in the snow. Zack didn't even remember the moment when Eric had shifted into a beast...or back.

Eric was also...hard. His cock was jutting out from his body, swollen with a blush on the tip that matched the one on the bridge of his nose. Eric snapped his hand down, trying to cover himself, but there was no way he could hide *that* behind his hand.

"Is it the bite?" asked Zack, honestly grasping at straws at this point. He could admit that the burn had simmered into a tingle, and in the right circumstances, it could be nice. He was still soft himself, even with the sight of everything that was Eric.

"The fight," said Eric, flushing even brighter and dipping his head, "and you. The smell of you is strong, but when your blood hit the air…" He licked his lips, his teeth looking alarmingly sharp as he slid his tongue over them.

"That is morbidly terrifying." Zack shifted so he could pull his feet under him. Eric had never hurt him before, but he looked so *hungry*. His eyes were wide, with the pupils pushing most of the gold to the edges. Even his hands were curled into fists as his cock visibly throbbed between his legs. There was no sign of the knot yet, but it was still intimidating.

Zack reached out to touch his palm to Eric's chest, not sure if he was going to push him away or usher him closer. Eric leaned into the touch, his eyes slitting as his hands relaxed.

"What can I do?" asked Zack. He owed everything to Eric. Eric had saved his life more than once, and he had given Zack the first taste of freedom—freedom from his curse. Now was not the time to be frightened, when he could finally offer him something in return.

"Let me kiss you?" asked Eric softly as he peered up through thick lashes. The way a man of his size and strength could be so shy still baffled Zack's mind. A kiss was not what he was expecting, either. He'd been ready to bare his neck and let the man take him in any way he wanted without regrets. It might be the last opportunity they would have together.

Zack surged ahead, planting his lips on Eric's and relishing his gasp. He slipped his tongue into the inviting cavern, sliding it along Eric's. There was a sharp tang to Eric's mouth that Zack belatedly realised was blood — the coyote's blood.

Zack slid his hands through Eric's hair, gripping the strands and pulling him closer while he lay back on the bed. Eric followed until he hovered his body over Zack's. The position should have been claustrophobic and stifling, but Zack had never felt more protected and whole. Eric's weight was perfect and feeling him between his thighs was even better.

They slid their bodies together, a rhythm building as Zack's cock came alive in his damp clothes. He moved to pull the snow-damp pants from his hips, but Eric was already there, moving his larger hands faster and stripping Zack to nothing. When their bodies touched again, there was nothing between them.

It was the first time they'd been like this without Eric trying to hide something. Zack wished he could have that back, so they could have done this so many times. Eric's cock against his sent a surge of lust into his belly like no other. And the touch of that heated, molten skin made him want to come.

"Fuck me," said Zack as he nibbled at Eric's lower lip, biting sharply as Eric groaned. He ached to have Eric inside him, almost more than the need to come. He couldn't count the number of ways he wanted him inside or how much he wanted to open Eric up and slide to the hilt, just to see how he would feel around his cock.

A spurt of pre-cum dribbled from Zack's cock as Eric growled, dropping down to Zack's neck and sinking his teeth into the skin. The bite was sharp, and probably broke skin, but Zack felt nothing but heat and pleasure. His darkness erupted and purred beneath the surface, simmering and fluttering in desire and seeming to enjoy the bite as much as Zack did.

"I can still smell him," Eric growled low again, dragging his nose over the Zack's flesh that was still sensitive from the bite. The touch sent his nerve endings firing, so much more sensitive than they should have been. If a simple bite could feel that good, Zack could only wonder what anything else would feel like.

"Claim me." The words were out of Zack's mouth before he could stop them. It was exactly what he wanted. To be claimed — wanted — and to finally find a home in the world. He pushed the thoughts of leaving to the back of his mind. He had to cherish this moment.

Eric dragged his tongue over the sensitive patch of skin and Zack bowed off the bed, his chest butting against Eric's. He gripped the back of Eric's head, twirling his fingers in his long hair.

"I said *claim* me," he demanded, his voice rough and leaving no room for a rebuttal.

A searing flash of heat split across Zack's flesh in the exact space that had burned so violently before. He could smell the tang of blood on the air, mixed with their sweat and the ever-present scent of pine. The heat spread down his body, all the way to his fingertips and toes, and the darkness surged beneath his skin as if it wanted to tear him apart. His head fell back, and he opened his mouth in silent awe as his breath fluttered from his lips. There was a steady growl coming from

Eric, so low that Zack barely registered it. He could feel it, though, vibrating against his chest.

"Fuck me, please, Eric," Zack begged before his breath was stolen again as Eric lined their cocks up and ground down. He felt like he could come in a heartbeat, but he was so empty. He needed Eric inside him more than he had ever needed anything before.

"Turn over," said Eric, grappling with Zack's hips, but slipping away as if he couldn't focus properly — as if he were as lost as Zack was.

"No," said Zack, stilling Eric's hands. "I want you like this, facing me. I want to watch you fall apart, and I want to see the look on your face when you come. You're so beautiful, Eric. Please let me see you."

Eric trembled as he looked at Zack with wide eyes. His lips were stained red, which was quickly wiped away with a pink tongue. He drew his brows together in apparent confusion as he chewed his lower lip.

"You think I'm beautiful?"

The question was so innocent, but it made Zack want to pummel everything and everyone that Eric had ever met.

"You are," said Zack, taking a deep breath to calm himself. "I mean, if I saw you in a bar, I would just drop to my knees on the dance floor and give you a BJ. If you invited me home, I would go. You are the most beautiful person I've ever seen."

Eric surged forwards, seeking Zack's lips and taking his breath. The copper taste was overwhelming as their tongues melded together again, but Zack managed to suppress his gag. It was just himself he was tasting, not anything else. It was just blood. A wave of queasiness made him pause.

It didn't matter. Eric was moving lower, sucking a finger into his mouth and dragging it over Zack's rim. He slicked it before pushing into Zack where he was still soft and ready. Zack groaned as he sank it all the way up to his last knuckle in one smooth movement.

"You're still soft for me," said Eric, looking surprised. "You were so tight last time, and I was so afraid that I would hurt you." He turned his hand and curled his finger skyward, sending Zack arching off the bed.

"If you weren't so hung, then I'm sure I'd be virgin-tight for you again," said Zack, gasping as his prostate was stroked to perfection. He usually was tight again pretty quick, sometimes needing a full stretch a few hours after a hump and bump. Eric's finger felt so hot inside him and his body was relaxing and opening so much easier.

Eric sank in a second finger, and Zack felt a twinge at his rim before he let out a breath and relaxed around the intrusion. Eric was barely giving his body time to catch up, his cock already dripping and slick, but Zack wasn't far behind. He was ready for a third finger before he had fully stretched for a second. He wanted Eric *now*.

"Another," Zack demanded, groaning when Eric listened without hesitation. There was none of the usual burn, only pure pleasure dancing along his nerves. Even with three fingers inside, Zack craved more, the ache in his belly throbbing.

After a final prod to his prostate, Eric withdrew with a slick slide that made Zack's toes curl. As much as he loved strawberry flavoured lube, spit was always so much better. He loved the natural slide that left nothing to the imagination. He could feel every ridge of his partner's knuckle and small scrape of his fingernail. When it started to dry, he revelled in the tug at his rim that made his toes curl.

His groan of loss was smothered against Eric's mouth as a blunt pressure pressed against his entrance. His cock was perfectly slick and sank in easily as Eric nudged against him. It should have hurt, but Zack only craved another inch as each one sank inside.

"Fuck me, fuck me," he chanted over and over as he wrapped his arms around Eric and tried to pull him close. The man was like a stone wall, refusing to budge or move any faster.

Not one to give up after a first try, he wrapped his legs around Eric, bringing his heels against Eric's buttocks and digging in for all he was worth. It was like trying to nudge a horse out of the way when there was a bucket of oats to be eaten.

Eric was moving so slowly—his eyes closed in concentration and his body trembling against Zack as if he were holding himself back. Zack didn't want him to, though. He wanted it all. But he had no leverage in this position on his back. He couldn't roll his hips with his legs wide, and Eric was too strong to be persuaded by force.

"Mount me." It was the only trump card Zack had, and he played it at the beginning of the hand. It worked like a charm.

Eric's eyes flew wide, and he snapped his hips forwards, burying himself to the base in one long thrust. He let out a growl that shook Zack's chest, and his lips curled back over his teeth, revealing red-stained canines that were too sharp to be human.

Zack squealed when Eric's cock thrust deeper than ever before. Even last time, the man had held back, not bottoming out for fear that Zack would discover his kinky secret.

"That feels like more than sixty percent," said Zack, taking a deep breath as he tried to relax around the massive cock inside him. His body had been screaming at him that he was ready when he obviously wasn't. He should have let Eric go slow, to avoid the brutal ache at the base of his spine, but no. Zack had had to be horny and cocky at the same time—a combination that would be sure to leave him aching for days...if not weeks.

Eric let out a small laugh, the feral look receding as his taut body relaxed. "I'd still only call that a solid eighty percent. My knot hasn't formed, and that's worth at least twenty." He chuckled and rolled his hips, the soft hair of his groin tickling against Zack's ass. Grabbing the back of Zack's knees, he pushed them wider and up until they were against Zack's chest and Eric was even deeper inside.

"Oh God," said Zack, biting his lower lip to keep the whine inside his chest back. "You're so fucking deep. Nothing's ever... I mean nobody... Fuck, I can't talk." Zack groaned as Eric's cock flexed inside, so hard and hot that it melted the ache away to nothing. He felt even deeper than the anal beads that Zack had shoved inside himself once. He didn't think the whole long string would really fit, despite his partner's insistence. If only they could see him now, with a cock inside that was almost as long as that string of beads.

"Don't worry," said Eric, kissing away Zack's groan as he ground against Zack's ass. "When my knot starts, I'll pull it out so I don't hurt you." He nipped at Zack's lower lip with a sear of heat.

"What? *No*," said Zack gripping Eric close and shaking his head. "I want it—your knot. I want you locked inside me so you can't pull out as you fill me up. Fuck, I want to be so full that I can't take another drop." The fantasy that had been brewing in the back of his mind was laid out in the open. He didn't know if it was possible, but he wanted to try, at least.

Eric let out a surprised gasp a moment before he seemed to lose control. He pulled out, leaving only an inch of his cock inside before he slammed forwards again, burying himself deep. Zack let out a yelp, followed by another when Eric did it again, harder than before. It was good, but it was also more than Zack could take. He'd never been so acutely aware of what his body could handle, and though he seemed to be able to accept Eric's cock, he definitely couldn't take it like a porn star.

"Slow, baby," Zack called out through another strangled yelp. He clamped his legs around Eric's hips, trying to force the man to stay buried deep. It never crossed his mind that he was calling a man twice his size 'baby'. "Fuck me slow, baby. Leave me wanting."

It was all he could say before Eric started to do just that. He lifted one of Zack's legs high, kissing his ankle as he rocked back. His thrusts quieted until they were gentle rolls that slowly built between each breath. Every slide was perfectly slick and filled Zack up to his absolute brim. Even the sound of it was beautiful, with their mixed gasps and heavy breaths, followed by the sound of slickness and the squeak of the bed as they shifted.

This wasn't mounting or fucking…or whatever Zack wanted to call it. This was slow and intimate, where the connection between them meant more than the happy ending. When Eric pushed Zack's knees back to his chest and leaned in for a breathless kiss, Zack finally realised what it was. *We're making love.*

His chest gripped tight as the pace quickened and something swelled against his rim. Eric's cock started to feel even bigger as the knot stretched Zack wider. He shot his hand down between them, jerking his cock quickly as Eric started to tremble.

Eric's lips crashed against his, and Zack was coming between them. He clamped down on the swelling cock within him as Eric bottomed out one last time. His body flexed as a groan pushed through his lips. Eric grew inside him, bigger than he could have imagined, then to the very point of pain as it pushed against his prostate.

It was so big that he could hardly breathe, and he knew that Eric would never be able to pull out. Tears sprang to his eyes as it kept growing, beyond anything his body was ever meant for. It was so much — too much — but then Eric started to come.

Heat that felt nearly boiling flowed inside him. He peaked again, clamping down on Eric a second time as he was filled.

With nowhere to go, Eric's cum rushed into him in the most wonderful way that had him instantly craving more. The ache of the knot receded to a steady overwhelming pressure that was better than any sex toy man had ever created. His body went lax as their breaths mingled and Eric eased some of his weight down onto Zack.

His back twinged from the position as Eric nuzzled as his neck, licking and biting the bruised column. The back of his leg was starting to cramp, and his ass cheek had a charley horse that was making itself known. The position they were in was great for fucking, but terrible for the after-fuck.

"So, how long are we stuck like this?" Zack asked, his voice much hoarser than he'd expected. He sounded so fucked-out, and his body agreed with that thought.

"Mm-m — an hour sometimes. I'm still coming now, so it might be longer," said Eric, his voice strained as another tremble went through his body.

"I'm not going to last that long," said Zack, trying to move his leg, but only succeeding at tugging at the knot inside him, making them both hiss.

As neat as the knot was, and as great as it felt, it seemed terribly inconvenient. What if they were attacked right now? He didn't want to imagine that thing pulling out of him when it felt that huge. He would never walk straight again.

"You wanted to face each other," mumbled Eric, continuing to bite at Zack's neck as if their conversation weren't any of his concern. "It's best from behind, but I was willing to try this. I admit, this is pretty great." He nipped as Zack's collar, obviously missing the scowl on Zack's face.

"Well, as glad as I am that I make a great pillow, please turn us around or something before my legs fall off." His other leg was starting to cramp, and his calf burned something fierce. How did porn stars do this? They would be in this position for a solid hour, and he never heard their complaints. Maybe all that was in the outtakes.

Eric chuckled, even as another shudder went through his body, and Zack felt a fresh wave of warmth inside. Of course, Eric was comfortable. He was still having his super-extended edition of an orgasm.

Eric leaned back slowly, careful not to tug at where they were joined. He grabbed Zack's leg, pushing it down to Zack's chest before trying to force it to the side, so Zack would have his legs together.

"Ow, fuck that stings when it tugs like that." Zack felt fresh tears heavy on his eyelashes as the knot moved inside him. The pressure on his sensitive prostate was beyond overwhelming, and the size of it made him shudder. Every time they moved, it felt like he was being ripped apart.

"If you would just..." Eric trailed off before he grabbed Zack's hips and dragged him to the edge of the bed.

"Motherfucker." Zack pinched Eric's nipple, making the demon gasp. "If you pull that hard again, I might break." His tailbone ached, and his ass burned so fucking much.

"Don't be a baby," said Eric as they reached the side of the bed.

"You're *my* baby," said Zack, grinning when Eric blushed and dipped his head. So Eric *had* heard him — and had liked it, apparently.

"I'm just going to turn you," said Eric, bracing them while crouching on the floor with Zack still on the bed. He grabbed Zack's leg again, reaching under him and gripping the opposite hip from behind.

"On three?"

"Just do it," said Zack. He cursed a moment later when Eric pulled his leg and his hip at the same time, effectively spinning him like a top so he was face down on the bed with Eric behind him. Eric's cock seemed to throb deeper as the knot tugged on his rim, threatening to pull out, even though it was impossible. A pile of aches assaulted him, and he took a deep breath.

"Note to self," said Zack, mumbling into the blanket. "Let the demon fuck you from behind." He stretched his legs out along Eric's hips, whimpering at the pull. Eric pressed down into him from behind, grinding his hips and rubbing his knot directly against Zack's prostate. It was nearly too much stimulation, but Zack's cock leaked as if he hadn't just come twice.

"Pillow," said Zack, looking up longingly at the pillow that was out of reach. This position couldn't be comfortable for Eric, who was perched over the side of the mattress and box spring like that.

Eric gripped Zack again, and lifted, moving them up the mattress.

"Ow, fuck. Stop doing that," said Zack, reaching back and smacking Eric's rumbling chest. "That really stung that time." He was aching now, and he couldn't imagine what it would feel like in an hour. Another wave of heat inside soothed him. He was so fucking full.

"Sorry," said Eric before he latched onto Zack's neck from behind, sinking into the same spot he had before. The coyote bite was nothing to how good this one felt, like every nerve was alive, yet singed.

"Shit," Zack ground back, forcing the knot against his bundle of nerves. He couldn't get hard again, but he felt like he was on the cusp of coming, his cock already leaking steadily. "Do it again."

Eric growled, his bite burning deeper as he snapped his hips forwards. Zack's vision whited out as he clamped down on Eric's cock, milking it for everything he was worth. The pleasure was fleeting, leaving him achy and completely sated.

Another wave of heat had his toes curling. Maybe this was going to be an hour-long wave of orgasms for him, too. He wasn't sure if he would survive.

"Can I feel it?" asked Zack, his voice rough as he reached down. Eric took his hand, guiding him to where they were connected.

The base of Eric's cock was narrow, holding Zack's hole only an inch-and-a-half or so wide, like a normal cock. He felt around his entrance, feeling the bulge of the knot beneath the skin, so hard and so big. When he edged forwards, just a bit, he could feel where the knot was trying to emerge, stretching him wide, but failing to pull free.

"It's big," said Zack, reaching farther down to Eric's sac. His sac felt so much lighter than it had before the man had come, all of it deep inside Zack. They were pulled up tight and firm against his palm.

"Are you still coming?" He fondled them in his hand, relishing Eric's gasp.

"Mm-mm maybe," he said, his laughter caught in a moan. "That feels good, Zack, keep doing that." He rocked his hips forwards, his knot slipping deep again.

Zack squeezed Eric's sac gently, rolling it in his hands and marvelling at the smoothness of the skin. For someone who turned into a beast, he didn't actually have a lot of body hair, and the hair he did have was soft. He stretched farther down, curling his body over so he could reach. Eric had grasped his hips again as he rutted inside.

Zack followed the seam on Eric's sac, then back farther to where he knew the man's entrance would be. His finger caught on the rim that was clenching rhythmically as Eric kept coming. He stretched farther, dipping the tip of his dry finger inside. He sank in smoothly, the slide slick as if he had coated himself in saliva.

"You're wet?" Zack pushed deeper before the stretch became too much and he had to pull away, straightening his body so his back was flush with Eric's chest again. "That's even more convenient than a wet cock." Lube would be a thing of the past as long as they went slow. The possibilities were endless.

Zack's stomach sank as he remembered that this would be the last time. He let his arms flop to the bed as he blinked away the tears that threatened to overflow. Why was he even crying? He'd known Eric for a few days, even if it felt like longer. He'd left others behind before.

"I'm not hurting you, am I?" Eric seemed to sense the change in Zack. He stopped nudging his hips, finally falling still. He loosened his grip on Zack's hips, trailing up and down his sides instead.

"No." Zack's voice wavered, and he bit his tongue, clearing his throat. "It's just more than I expected." He didn't expect the rush of emotions barraging his chest and he didn't expect guilt to come and ram him in the guts either.

"It's perfect," said Eric, so low that Zack didn't think he was supposed to hear.

It really was perfect—the stretch inside, filling him more than he thought possible, and Eric's hands on him, so warm and comforting. Every place that Eric had bitten him was warm and itchy like a muscle after a good workout. He felt claimed and wanted.

"I've never gone slow like that before," Eric said louder, kissing the sensitive spot behind Zack's ear and making him shudder. "With the demons and were-animals I've been with, it's usually quick and...

efficient. Sometime the knot is the only thing that keeps them, or me, from leaving and carrying on the rest of the day."

"And the humans you've been with?" asked Zack, pushing away the jealousy as he thought of Eric with someone else—an ass like Jared, or some other bitch looking for a quick fuck.

"You're the only one… I've never wanted another human before. Humans are…" He trailed off as if he were realising for the first time that it was a human in his arms. "Sorry."

"I get it," said Zack, feeling a flush of warmth at the thought of being the only person in Eric's life. "People can be different sometimes. Some of the people I've met would do best behind bars or six feet under. But there are good people, too, a lot more good ones than bad. Don't let one bad one ruin it for everyone."

"It's not that there were bad ones," said Eric, squeezing Zack tighter. "I haven't even spoken to a human in years. If one finds their way back here, I just disappear and wait for them to leave. I've never helped one out of the snow before, but something felt different with you. The wind changed the night you got stuck on the road and something drew me out there. When I saw you, freezing in that car with no socks on and a spring jacket, I knew I had to help you. Then, when I smelled you for the first time, I thought it was some kind of trap—something sent by another legion."

"And you let me stay, anyway?" Zack desperately wanted to see Eric's face, but they were still stuck together with Eric's knot throbbing inside him and gently tugging against his aching rim.

"It was nice to see someone else cleaning up this cabin," Eric laughed, "and I couldn't resist you."

They fell into silence as Zack's mind whirled. Eric made it sound like they were some kind of fated pair, destined to meet on the errant winds of the world. He made it sound like this wasn't supposed to be temporary.

Eric let out a soft sigh, and Zack felt something shift inside him. A moment later, Eric was tugging free with a rush of cum that made Zack blush and slap a hand against his face.

"I don't mind a little cream-pie action in porn," said Zack, refusing to look up as he continued to leak, "but that's the whole fucking pie."

Chapter Sixteen

Snow crumbled under Zack's feet as he pushed through it, pulling his tattered jacket around his shoulders. The trees reflected the sound of his footsteps back to him like a rhythmic and listless echo.

Every step added another layer of agony. Even his dick ached from so many consecutive orgasms. His ass was worse — so, so much worse. He felt like he'd fucked a watermelon, and he was still leaking a bit of the juice.

It made him flush each time he felt a bit of cum seep between his cheeks. Eric had left his mark and then some, and Zack felt completely claimed, despite the fact that he was walking away from the cabin.

He'd left Eric after they'd cleaned up, and he'd fallen asleep on the stained bed. Zack had forced himself to stay awake, slipping into as many layers as he could before he stepped out into the night. He'd left his car behind, knowing that the sound of the engine would wake Eric. There was no way he could get it out of the pile of snow before dawn, anyway.

He'd seen a few cars before he had managed to get stuck in the storm. Most of them were four-wheel-drive pick-ups that put his two-door to shame. But men with pick-ups were either country singers or rednecks, at least in Zack's experience. Neither of those groups would have a problem picking him up on the side of the road. He only hoped he made it to the road with his feet still attached, and that a truck came by before dawn, so he didn't have to wander all night.

He walked for what felt like nearly an hour, his feet freezing and his body sweating as he ploughed through the drifts. Eric had definitely dragged his car to the cabin. There was no way he could have driven through some of the drifts, and there were a few places where trees had mysteriously toppled for no apparent reason, their seeping sap still fresh and vibrant. Zack knew that Eric was strong but seeing that, and remembering how quickly he'd returned, was another thing entirely.

The forest finally parted, revealing a moon-lit stretch of pavement that was slick with thick ice. The sky was so clear, and the moon was shining so brightly, that he had to squint as he looked at it. It was almost like a spooky version of midday.

Deliberating for a moment, he turned left, back the way he had originally come days before. He stayed at the border of snow and ice where he didn't have to trudge too deeply. The ploughs had definitely been by, but they must have run out of salt at some point. The edges were still solid and slippery, but there was a thin pathway of slush that soaked through his shoes in seconds. Hopefully, there would be someone as crazy as him on the road soon.

His sweat had dried, leaving only damp coolness behind by the time the first set of headlights carved into his skull. He blinked dumbly, like a deer caught in the light, before he stepped to the side and into the deeper snow. He raised his hand, his heart pounding as the car approached, but didn't slow.

The car whipped past him, throwing a tuft of snow into his face as the tyres spun. He spluttered, wiping the snow from his face and throwing up his middle finger at the retreating vehicle. The dark cab obscured the driver, but he was almost certain that it contained a conceited asshole.

Three more vehicles whipped by him in the next five minutes, every one throwing a face full of snow his way as he trudged along. His feet were soaked, and his fingers felt like they would fall off the next time he pulled his hands from his pockets.

The plan had sounded so much better in his head, than it did in practice. *Hit the road, hitchhike to the nearest town and crash at a motel.* He still had his trust fund, as much as he loathed it. Hopefully the cops hadn't frozen the account to try to track him down. That was, if they knew who he was. He'd never given his ex his last name.

He shuffled to a stop, slush brimming at the edge of his shoes. He didn't have any cash left. What the hell was he going to do if the account was locked? Turn himself in? That would last until the first inmate tried to come at him. It wouldn't hurt, not after taking Eric's knot up his ass, but he wasn't keen on rape, even if the guy did get fried by his curse a few seconds into it. It would just add another body to his growing tally.

A throaty rumble caught his attention a moment too late. He slipped in the icy slush, his feet sliding to the side as he face-planted into the slop. Headlights blinded him on the way down, sending sparks into his vision as he braced for impact. He heard the squeal of brakes and the chuff of anti-lock on ice before the engine kicked down to a purr.

"What the hell are you doing out there?" a deep voice screamed at Zack as someone stepped out of the cab of an obtusely large pick-up. The light obscured his face, leaving only a silhouette and spots dancing in front of Zack's eyes.

"Just thought I would go for a stroll," Zack bit out as he pulled a pebble from between his teeth. The face plant had smooshed a wonderful amount of gravel and grit into his mouth, topped with salt. The ploughs had salted after all, but it was just so fucking cold out that the slush had started to freeze again.

"I didn't hit you," the stranger barked as he drew closer. It wasn't a question, but an accusation, as if Zack had his lawyer perched in the woods, waiting for the best time for a lawsuit.

"Nope, but that probably would have made my day," said Zack, blinking up at the light. His patience had officially expired, and it was just his luck that the only person to stop was an asshole. Where was his country-singing hero? Probably sitting by the fire and not out in the snow.

"I just need to get to town." Zack squinted, trying to get a good look at the guy's face, but failing in the shadows. He saw plaid and a beard...*wonderful*. "My car broke down about a three-hour walk that way." He pointed over his shoulder back the way he'd come.

"I'm not taking you anywhere," plaid-man grumbled, kicking at an ice-covered tyre. "I don't know you, and I've never seen you before. We get folks up here sometimes, ones that are runnin' from the law. You a criminal, boy?"

What would be the best response? He was a criminal, but not by choice. This guy probably had a shotgun in the cab of his truck from his general attitude. He sounded like he only had one tooth left in his head as well. A wonderful redneck reception overall.

"Can I borrow your phone then? I'll call a tow," he said, grasping at straws. He would probably be able to convince the tow truck driver to take him to town.

Zack scraped the last of the slush from his jacket and legs. It had seeped in, leaving him even colder than before. The wet and filthy strands of his hair were quickly clumping and freezing together.

He bent down to tie the lace on his sneaker that had come undone while he was making love to the road. The last thing he wanted was another mouthful of gravel. The road was quiet beyond the grumbling engine, the highway clear of any other traffic.

There was a sickening squelching sound and a soft grunt that had Zack looking up from his shoe. The silhouette of the man had disappeared, the headlights shining directly at him in a way that made his eyes burn. He blinked the spots from his vision, spying a stain on the snow.

His heart pounded in his ears. It wasn't a stain at all. The snow around him had been flawless other than the slush. This imperfection was new, and it was spreading. He could see a wisp of steam that rose from it against the headlight. The smell of it hit him a second later, a smell that he was all-too familiar with.

Blood.

Chapter Seventeen

"We knew you would come out sometime, little bitch," a voice called from beside him, where the trail of blood dripped off the side of the road. "No one is around to protect you now, are they?"

Zack stumbled to his feet, trying to see into the darkness, but failing miserably. The headlights did nothing but blind him to everything but the snow beneath his feet. He knew the voice, and it was one that he had expected to hear from again, but not so soon. He was supposed to be far from there by the time the demons caught up. Eric said he had weeks, not hours.

Zack's heart nearly stopped when he heard laughter, hot with the stench of blood and something putrid.

"He looks so scared, Simon. What do you think? The bitch didn't think we would just stick around and take him out as soon as he stepped off Coy-Boy's land. We didn't know that the half-breed had that kind of power, but he can't help you out here." A naked foot moved into the beam of light, a barely clothed leg following.

Zack felt the darkness shiver under his skin, but there was something wrong. It was out of his reach, barely a whisper of what it usually felt like, as if the power had drained from him. He could almost see the tether, stretched thin and reaching for Eric.

He was vulnerable for the first time in his life, and Eric couldn't save him. The first time it actually mattered, and he was fucking powerless.

A second laugh sounded off to Zack's left from within the darkness. They stepped into the light. It was the two from before, their eyes deep black and looking no worse for wear. The one to his left, the larger of the two, was dripping blood from his hands to his elbows. It didn't look like it belonged to him.

"I don't know, Phil," said the one on his left—Simon. "Maybe the bitch did know, and he wanted to have some fun. He's not exactly running." His head tilted to the side, his black eyes fathomless pits in the dark. His bronze body shimmered under the light of the moon.

Simon took a step closer, his breath tainting the air. His blood-stained hand slid over Zack's shoulder, sinking into the shell of Zack's jacket. The stain spread, tainting the repaired fabric forever.

Zack's mind whirled, dragging so sluggishly that he wanted to scream. That simple touch on his shoulder felt worse than a violation, but he didn't have a choice. He was so weak.

Zack leaned into the touch, nodding even as his heart pounded in his chest. "Out of the demons I've met, you guys look like you take the least steroids—at least an eight...except Phil." Zack looked over at the second figure as he approached. "Phil is more like a seven-and-a-half."

Who was Zack kidding? Other than their creepy-ass eyes and their blood-stained hands, they were both solid tens out of tens on the hotness scale. Threatening rape, definitely knocked them down a few pegs. If they'd met in different circumstances, they might have made for a good time, but guys who didn't take no for an answer, were the lowest of the low.

"What are you talking about?" Simon murmured as he stepped in behind Zack, leaning over to run his nose over his chilled neck. Zack pulled his collar tight, the thin fabric protecting him from the unwanted touch.

"It's a scale," said Zack, clenching his hands so he didn't try to push Simon away. "It rates how hot a guy is — or how fuckable they are." He failed to suppress a shudder as Simon wrapped his arms around his waist, pulling him back against a bulge that he had no interest in ever touching.

"What's it out of?" Simon chuckled, nosing at Zack's collar before peeling it down, his freezing nose sliding over Zack's flesh. The touch felt so wrong, just like the coyote's had, only frigid instead of burning. "Uh, you reek of him."

"It's out of a hundred," said Zack. He hoped he reeked of Eric. He hoped they could smell Eric's cum that was still leaking out of him and dripping on the inside of his pants. The touch against the sensitive edge of Eric's bite felt worse than an ice cube against his skin.

"Play nice, little bitch. You wouldn't like to see us upset," teased Phil, moving forwards until he was against Zack's front. They were both solid walls of muscle, Zack more than a full head shorter than their bulk, and much narrower. He expected some heat from their bodies, or something to stave off the building wind, but they weren't like Eric at all. They were cold everywhere Eric was boiling.

There was no way out, and nothing Zack could do. His darkness was muted like the winter storm around them, and there was no one coming to his rescue. Eric would still be sleeping in his bed, completely unaware that Zack was even gone, and there were no yellow eyes shining from the ditch. Eric had finally managed to scare his brother off, too.

"Can you shut that truck off, Phil? I don't want anyone pulling over to see what's going on," said Simon, his grip relaxing as he looked up and down the road. His posture was still, his body a line of tension against Zack's back. "Get rid of the body, too."

"Are you afraid?" asked Zack, a sudden realisation surfacing. Phil turned away from them, touching his hand to the front of the truck until it spluttered to a halt, the whole frame trembling in protest as the engine stalled out.

"Of you? No. You're the one who should be afraid, bitch." Simon's voice lowered to a murmur that made every hair on Zack's body stand up. "When we are finished with the fun that Jared promised, we'll turn you over to our leader. I'm sure he would be happy to have something like you in his possession…whatever you are." He took another deep breath before he let out a low chuckle.

"I see Coy-Boy already managed to sink his teeth into you. Predators are such silly creatures. They have no idea how to make something like you submit." He touched the edge of the bite, sending a trickle of ice down Zack's spine.

"I have an idea," said Zack, wiggling until Simon loosened his grip enough for him to whirl around. He couldn't let the demon touch the spot that Eric had marked. The patch of skin felt almost sacred, and right now, it was being defiled in the worst way.

He kept his body relaxed, dipping his head down in a way that he hoped would show his submission. "Just you, though. I don't want to share." Zack looked up through his lowered lashes and smoothed his tongue along his lower lip. His mouth was dry, and his tongue tugged instead of sliding smoothly.

Simon's lips curled into a smile—his wide, flat teeth just visible in the moon's bright glow. It was easier to see now with the headlights no longer blinding them. The moon looked bigger and brighter than before, with every star at its back in unyielding support.

"Come with me," said Simon, pulling at Zack's hand as he turned in the direction of the forest.

"No, here," said Zack. "The snow is too deep for me to walk through, and it's so cold." He grasped Simon's hand and pulled him back, the demon surprisingly not resisting. The snow *was* too deep—too deep to run through to try and escape. The demons thought he was powerless, so he knew they wouldn't put up a fuss. Hopefully, like him, they thought with their dicks more than their heads.

"Take off, Phil," said Simon, waving off his friend's splutter and turning his focus back to Zack. "I'll take our filly for a spin, and I'll come get you when it's time for your turn."

"But...just you," said Zack, his voice wavering as Phil disappeared into the snow and the darkness of the trees, his footsteps silent against the wind. He took a step forwards, forcing himself to lean against Simon's body, shivering from the touch.

"It's okay. I'll take good care of you." Simon's hands squeezed him in a grip that felt like it was supposed to be comforting. It made his skin crawl instead.

Zack took a deep breath to centre himself. There was one saving grace if his plan failed. Eric seemed to have some qualities from his beast, even when he looked human — his knot being one of those. If these men were anything like the horses had been on his grandpa's farm, they were bound to be two-pump chumps. At least it wouldn't be drawn out for too long.

Gripping Simon's shoulders and tilting his head to look into those dark, soulless eyes, Zack brought his knee up as hard as he could. He'd taken a self-defence course after a few close calls and one bad experience. He knew exactly how to twist his body to make the blow hit with the most impact, and he remembered how to aim directly for the goods.

The blow was strangely silent, and so was the wheeze from Simon's mouth. The man had been hard, from what Zack had felt, which would have only made the blow that much worse for him. A blow like that would have Zack mourning his never-going-to-happen-great-grandchildren and spending the rest of his life in a wheelchair.

Simon hit the ground on both knees, his hands dropping to protect his squished package that would never be the same again. He let out another wheeze, hunching forwards until his face hit the ground, rubbing a line of slush against his cheek.

Zack scrambled back, looking for anything to protect himself. The truck was still there, the engine cooling and useless with the demon so close. The driver had seemed like the type who would have a crowbar in his truck, or a gun… Hell, even a snowbrush would be fine.

He scrambled to the door, pulling it open and jumping into the back seat. Scraping his hand over the floor, he searched in the dark for anything that could help him. His hand hit something metal, and he grabbed it before he stumbled back and out of the truck.

He caught sight of what was in his hand as the moonlight hit it. He'd seen it before but couldn't remember what it was called. It was shaped like a cross, with a spot on one end to place a tyre's bolt for tightening. The thing that mattered was that it was as heavy as hell.

Zack wasn't sure when he had stopped valuing the unique contribution that each individual life made in the world. Maybe it was around the time that one of his lovers had ended up impaled by a tree branch or when his family had started to fear him, even if they didn't know why.

He didn't know when it had come to this — or how he could deliberately attack someone, or something with every intention of killing them. He'd thought he was a nice guy, or at least a decent one, but decent guys didn't swing a tyre iron at someone's head. Decent guys didn't hit them a second time when they were down, watching their dark blood flow in the moonlight.

He lost count of the hits and the number of times that *something* splattered against his face, mixing with his cooling tears. He only stopped when the iron slipped from his wet fingers, thudding to the ground. His knees hit the slush next, but he could hardly feel the cold.

The demon lay still, its last breath long gone. He'd done it again. Over and over like a haunting mantra, but this time, it really was his fault. The blood on his palms was sticky and thick, making him gag until his dinner mingled with the filth on the road.

Apparently, he had a knack for it. Whether it was luck or fucking fate, he wasn't sure.

When the sun peaked over the tips of the trees, there was a body on the ground beside him. Phil hadn't returned after Simon had sent him away, but maybe he had seen the carnage and fled.

Zack knelt there, waiting for the next car to drive by and to finally notice the massacre. But the road had been silent ever since the stranger had pulled over with the refusal to help him.

He was still on his knees, his shaking long-since stopped when Eric found him.

Chapter Eighteen

"I'm going to get more water," said Eric, speaking in a low, soothing voice as he squeezed Zack's hand. His face wavered in and out as tears, water and filth flowed over Zack's open eyes, trailing a line of sludge into them. He wasn't sure if the water was boiling or if his skin was just that cold, but he could hardly stand it.

When he'd stripped naked and stepped into the shower, his clothes had stuck to him, leaving imprints behind that he didn't want to look at. He could still smell it, stuck in his nostrils, even after the water had started to run clear. His clothes were gone, along with his coat and his shoes. Eric had taken them all with a grim look, before he had tossed them outside to be burned.

"Zack, look at me." Eric's voice wavered as Zack weaved where he stood. He thought he would still be able to see him — the person he had…killed. He should have been able to see their face, etched forever in his memory.

There was nothing. Now that the blood was gone, he barely remembered what it had looked like on his hands. Had it ever been there at all?

The smell was the only thing that was still clinging, but other things were starting to overwhelm that. There was Eric, and pine and the mild scent of homemade soap creeping in, taking the last of stench.

The darkness buzzed under his skin as if it had never left. When Eric had finally discovered he was missing, it had grown beneath his skin. With each step, his curse had flared to life, somehow tied to the only man who had ever shown him freedom.

"Did I?" Zack asked as he peered up from his clean hands. Eric was there, hovering over him as he sank to his knees. "How could I?" His vision blurred as a sob broke from his chest. Eric touched him, a heat so vibrant that it scalded his skin.

"It wasn't your fault," said Eric, his grip hardening until Zack sobbed, his teeth chattering as his body shook.

"I'm pretty sure it was my fault. I took the thing— don't know what it was called. It was so heavy and solid. What happens when someone finds him?" Zack's heart started to pound. The demon was laying out there, waiting for the next watchful eye.

"The human is taken care of. They hid him well enough that there will be nothing left by the time he's found. As for the demon, he will fade, the same way we all do." He paused, wrapping his arms around Zack and pulling him close, his scent enveloping. "Demons can only take from the world. We can't give anything back. He will simply fade as if he were never here in the first place. His body will melt into the snow, and his blood will wisp away on the wind. It was already starting when I found you, and he should be gone by the time anyone finds the truck. I pushed it off the road to give us more time."

The one murder he had deliberately committed, and the evidence had disappeared into nothing. Zack probably wasn't supposed to feel relieved, but he did. He wanted to laugh and cry at the same time. He couldn't blame himself for the driver. In fact, if he had killed the demon sooner, the driver would still be alive, and Zack would have been in a far-away town.

"One got away," said Zack, returning Eric's hug and letting his tears dry from his skin. "Simon told him to leave, so we could… Well, he was going to try to force me…but he never came back. I didn't want to do that. Not again." Zack had hung around too many assholes. No one should ever be forced once in their life, let alone twice.

"They can't force you, Zack. It's okay. Take a deep breath for me," said Eric, rubbing a molten hand down Zack's naked back. "It's just like the bite. If you didn't want it, not even a little bit, then it would hurt him as much as his touch hurt you. We can't leave anything behind, Zack. Nothing for ourselves that isn't for someone else. That goes for children, too. Our biology doesn't understand the difference between men and women, but it's the same. If he tried to fuck you without you wanting it, his cock would have felt like it was about to freeze off."

"His nose felt so cold," said Zack, shivering at the memory. "Why would he even try? If it would hurt him so much, he should have just killed me." He reached for the back of his neck where Eric's bite was. The skin was hot and so sensitive.

"I don't think they wanted to kill you, Zack. They can be very…convincing. He would have persuaded you. We're good at that." Eric's face darkened as he looked over his shoulder, grabbing another bucket of scalding water and pouring it into the watering can with one hand so he didn't have to let go of Zack. He only left for a moment to lift the can onto the hook.

Eric was clothed, but he was soaked to the bone, every line of his sculpted body on display through the wet fabric.

"They convinced you," said Zack, already knowing the answer. The water steamed as it hit him, finally starting to sooth the persistent ache.

"Like I said, we are very convincing." Eric's mouth lifted into a small smile that didn't reach his eyes. He grabbed a cloth from the floor, rubbing a persistent stain from Zack's belly.

"You aren't like them," said Zack, reaching for Eric's hand as the demon lowered his gaze. "You gave me freedom, and that's worth more to me than anything."

"I *am* like them, Zack," said Eric as he pulled away. "I may only be half-demon, but I'm exactly like them. You can feel it, can't you? When I claimed you, I bound you to me somehow. When you leave, you'll be free of your curse."

Zack knew exactly what Eric was talking about. His curse — his darkness — the bane of his fucking existence, was buzzing under his skin, stronger than ever. When he'd run away from Eric, he had hardly felt it. He had almost felt…normal.

"But I want to stay," said Zack. He listened to the words as they came out of his mouth, not sure if he had heard correctly. Did he really want to stay in a place with no Wi-Fi, no heat, no water and enough snow that a body could be literally lost on the front porch?

He wanted a shower that lasted more than five minutes, that came out of a tap and not a can. He wanted to sleep on a bed that had an actual frame. And mostly, he wanted to cruise social media for no particular reason other than to find cute cat videos.

But Eric was *here*.

"Maybe you could come with me?" said Zack, reaching for Eric's chin and tilting his head up to meet his gaze. He gasped, falling back when he found black, soulless eyes that drew the warmth from the room.

"I can't leave, Zack. There would be…consequences if I did. This is it until the end for me — until there is nothing left but a crumbling cabin in the middle of nowhere." He blinked, black burning away to gold.

Well, if that wasn't the most depressing thing that Zack had ever heard in his life, he wasn't sure what was. "Wouldn't you get bored? I mean, there is literally nothing to do here but eat, fuck and chop wood." Zack looked down at the swirling water that gathered around his knees. He looked so clean, as if nothing had happened at all. But his chest was still tight.

"And hunt." Eric's gaze darkened before he turned away to reach for a towel, wrapping it around Zack's shoulders. "I know you mean well, Zack, and I've enjoyed our time together. I'll push your car out to the road tomorrow so you can leave. The roads are clear, and you should be able to get out before the next storm comes."

"I've worn out my welcome, then?" Zack gripped the towel, suddenly feeling much colder. The towel was so threadbare that he wouldn't be surprised if it was older than him. It was covered in stains that had faded over time, but it smelled fresh, like the laundry he had slaved away at. A single thread at the corner threatened to unravel the entire thing.

"Could I visit? I mean, I'll probably pass this way again. I travel around a lot, but maybe I can settle somewhere close by." Once he cleared up things with the cops, that was. He might just end up behind bars, but he could visit once he got parole.

"If I ever saw you again, I would never be able to let you leave," Eric turned away, stripping the soaked shirt from his shoulders and throwing it towards the fire. It landed at the base of the hearth with a wet splat, a few drops of water sizzling against the flames.

"I don't understand. Do you want me to stay or leave?" Zack stood, suddenly feeling very vulnerable in just a towel. It hadn't mattered before, when Eric had scrubbed the filth from his body.

"I want you to have a choice." Eric rounded on him, his shoulders hunched and his voice a low growl. "I can be very convincing, Zack, just like them. I won't take that choice away from you. You have to get out of here while you still can."

Chapter Nineteen

They lay on the bed next to each other, but Zack couldn't have felt farther apart. It was only a double bed, but they were each on opposite edges, perching on the sides as if the centre of the bed were made of lava. Eric's back was to him, a hunched impenetrable wall that only moved with each breath. He wasn't sleeping. There was no way that someone could sleep with their shoulders up around their ears like that.

The blanket was much too small for the both of them lying so far apart. Zack had tried to hand it over, despite the chill to the room, but Eric had turned away, pushing it behind him. The smell of Eric, so strong and dark, nearly smothered Zack as he brought the fur up to his chin. Despite the fire, the room was freezing, and Zack's toes ached from his march through the snow.

He'd tried to say goodnight, but Eric had ignored him. Every time Zack had tried to speak to the demon throughout the day, he'd been met with the slam of the cabin door and a burst of cold air as Eric stormed out. A part of him wanted to leave then, while it was still light outside, and he had the whole day to put space between them. But he was so tired that he could barely keep his eyes open. It had nothing to do with the way his chest ached fiercely when he looked out to see his car.

Eric had uncovered it, digging it out of the drift to expose the bald tyres and rusted frame. It was ready to go, and Zack had a bag packed with borrowed clothes.

Not borrowed. He would never return them. They were just another thing to add to his stolen collection.

"Are you going to ignore me for the rest of the night?" Zack asked into the still room, unable to take the tension any longer. Eric flinched at his words, even as his breaths stayed even and low. "I know you aren't sleeping, Eric." He tugged the blanket higher, ducking into its warmth. "I can hear you grumbling from here. I can't sleep knowing that the other one, Phil, is still out there. What if he's waiting for me?" In truth, Zack wasn't worried at all. He'd taken out two, supposedly all-powerful, demons already. What was one more?

"You don't need to worry about him. A lone demon like him, one that has lost his cohorts, will be turned away or taken out. No one will come for you." The words were quiet, the line of muscling on Eric's shoulder bulging. It looked like the man was grabbing the worn fitted sheet to keep himself from striking out or rolling over.

"Good to know," Zack mused, shuffling a tiny bit closer so he could toss the lowest part of the blanket over Eric's feet. "Then what about you? How do I know you won't come after me?" He played with the short strands of fur on the blanket. He wanted Eric to come after him. *No.* He wanted Eric to come with him.

"I won't," said Eric, his shoulders shaking from the strain. Zack could feel the heat from his body, as if the fire was in the bed and not in the hearth.

"What if —?"

"Stop." The words were dipped in a deep growl that made every hair on Zack's body stand up. Eric had never sounded so much like a predator before. Zack felt around for his self-preservation, but it had obviously checked out, because his heart was steady.

"No," said Zack as he tossed the blanket back and reached for Eric. Heat seared under his palm as he touched Eric's shoulder, so fierce that he fell back. His hand felt like it should have blistered from the temperature, but there was nothing, only agony.

"Fuck," Zack grunted and bent over his arm, cradling it to his chest. The pain was fading so fast that it left his fingertips numb and his palm feeling like he was holding fresh snow. It was the same way that the coyote's bite had felt when Zack had rejected him.

Eric didn't want him there. He truly didn't. And he didn't want to be touched.

Zack stumbled out of bed, pulling on the nearest pair of pants, which happened to be loose joggers that were too big to stay up on their own. He cranked on the draw string, pulling it as tight as he could before struggling to tie it with his shaking hands. He blinked back tears while scrambling for the nearest shirt, nearly sobbing when Eric's scent engulfed him.

"What are you doing?" asked Eric as he sat up on the bed, naked except for a thin pair of shorts. His skin gleamed in the firelight, every groove and muscle stark against the grim shadows that were painted behind him. His eyes were black.

"Leaving." His voice was thin and high, making it obvious that he was seconds from crying. He'd never wanted to stay anywhere before. He had hoped that Eric had felt the same, but Zack was deluding himself. He was obviously just another notch on the demon's bed post...not that he had a bedpost. Just another way to pass the boredom of his monotony.

"But...morning," said Eric, staggering from the bed. Gold burned away the black emptiness of his eyes, leaving him bare and open. He raised his hands, reaching for Zack, but unable to close the distance.

Zack wanted to lean into the touch, but he also didn't want the same agony that he'd experienced before. "You don't want me here, and you don't want me. I can go, just like you asked. You won't hear from me again."

Zack turned to the door, a lump settling into his gut. He sniffed and pinched the base of his nose to stave off his tears. He could last until he got outside. It was only a few steps, then he would be free, and the world would be his to explore.

Alone.

"Wait. Please," said Eric. He settled his hand on Zack's shoulder, spreading the most exquisite warmth that drove away all thoughts of winter and ice. "I don't want you to leave. Not tonight. Please stay. I can't... I can't bear to lose you, Zack. Not yet. Please, just give me one more night."

Zack took a step back until he pressed against the warmth of Eric's chest. He was solid, and so strong, like a wall of lean muscle and corded strength. His smoky scent thickened with the tears on Zack's cheeks, wrapping him in a blanket of acceptance — even if it was only for a moment.

Eric's breath tickled the back of his neck as the demon pulled him close. As Zack shifted, he could feel the man against his ass, soft, but still firm. He knew what it felt like inside him, and he wanted it again.

Maybe just one more time.

"It burned when I touched you," said Zack, looking down at his hand. It looked normal, as if nothing had ever happened. As if the nerves had never been stripped raw and pressed to a naked flame.

"I didn't mean to hurt you. I thought if I touched you again, I wouldn't be able to let you go. You can't stay here, Zack. There's no life for you here, but out there, where I can't go, there's so much for you there. You can live a normal life now. Your curse is bound to me, and the farther you go, the better."

"I want to stay," said Zack, gripping the hands pressed to his chest. "Don't let me go." He bit back a sob, refusing to break down any further than he already had.

"I have to, and you have to let me go, too, Zack. You have to live on and forget about me. This cabin can only be a memory to you, and you…you can never be more than the one that got away." He kissed the back of Zack's neck, over the vivid claim mark that made Zack's cock fill.

"Let me have you tonight," said Zack, turning in Eric's arms. He lifted himself up on the balls of his feet, cradling Eric's face in his hands before bringing their lips together. Eric's lips were so soft, so warm and so utterly perfect under Zack's that he just wanted to kiss this man for the rest of his life. Eric parted for him, and he pushed inside, delving deep and tasting everything that the demon had to offer. Their tongues danced together, neither fighting for dominance, just embracing each other.

Zack groaned, sliding his hands through Eric's thick, soft hair and pulling Eric down to him, asking the man to take control. He simply followed Zack's lead, sucking his tongue into his mouth and feasting on him.

"Take me to bed," said Zack as he nipped Eric's lip hard enough to bruise. The demon groaned, dropping his hands to squeeze Zack's ass and kneading the globes in his broad palms. Without seemingly any effort at all, he lifted Zack, pulling him close so Zack could wrap his legs around him and bring their groins together.

In a few steps, they were at the bed. Zack expected to be lowered down, so Eric could cover his body and grind down from above. Instead, Eric sat on the edge of the mattress, the corner dipping under their combined weights as Zack shifted in Eric's lap.

From this position, Zack was the one with the advantage. Eric was stronger, but Zack had height on his side and the willingness of the demon beneath him.

Endless opportunities stretched out before him. He could imagine sliding into Eric's excruciating heat and feeling the demon clench around him with the perfect pressure. His cock throbbed as he thought about pushing Eric's knees to his chest, exposing where they were connected, and looking at his tight hole stretched around his cock.

"Can I?" Zack asked, dipping his lips to Eric's rugged jawline and revelling in the scratch of two-days of growth against his lips. Eric's pulse rabbited under his lips as he kissed down his neck, sucking a bruise in the spot under his ear. Eric groaned, grinding up and clenching Zack's ass until Zack knew he would have bruises in the morning.

"Whatever you want," said Eric after a second gasp as Zack nibbled on the hollow of his throat.

Zack pushed at Eric's shoulders, easing the man back on the bed. With a few quick manoeuvres, they were in the middle, with Eric's head comfortably nestled back against a pillow. Zack could feel the excruciatingly hard length beneath his ass twitch as he ground down, trying to catch his breath as his heart pounded. He wanted this man so much, and he was going to have him in every way that he could.

He kissed his way back down to Eric's neck, dragging his teeth over the sensitive column. Eric groaned and bucked hard enough that Zack almost rolled off him. The demon seemed to have an absolute obsession with biting, and it didn't seem to matter whether it was giving or receiving.

Zack bit down, hard enough that he knew there would be an impression of his teeth, but not enough to break skin. Eric bucked again, groaning as he threaded his fingers through Zack's hair, pulling him closer.

"Harder. Bite me," said Eric, whining as Zack complied.

Zack had never really bitten anyone, at least, not enough to attempt to break skin. His teeth felt too dull to pull it off, and his jaw ached from the strain. It didn't seem possible that he could break skin—until he did.

He gasped as Eric flooded into his mouth, letting out a sound that was trapped between pain and euphoria. The taste wasn't terrible…not the copper bitterness that he'd been expecting…but another version of smoke and pine—Eric's true essence. His teeth tingled and he felt his darkness surge under his skin, licking where his mouth was pressed to Eric and where his palms braced against his chest.

Eric writhed, a scream coming from his mouth that was from anything but pain. His eyes were wide, gold pushed to the edges as his pupils blew wide. He looked thoroughly intoxicated, and Zack had barely started.

He dug his teeth in harder, gnawing at the skin and sucking at the sweetness that flooded over his tongue. When his jaw started to ache too much to bear, he probed each indent with his tongue, swiping at every place that his teeth had carved into the beautiful flesh. It healed under his tongue, so fast that he mourned the loss. But his jaw was too sore to bite again with the same strength, and Eric sounded close to hysteria already.

When he pulled back, there was nothing left except slightly reddened skin that was shiny with spit. There wasn't even a scar, even though the taste of Eric still burned over his tongue. Eric's face was flushed, and the rosiness spread all the way down his chest. His nipples were peaked, begging to be touched.

Zack moved down, dragging his teeth over Eric's neck one last time before he dipped lower. The ache in his jaw was already fading, and he wanted to make Eric moan again like his world would end if he didn't come.

He licked into the hollow of Eric's throat, sucking the sweat and pine from his skin. He skimmed his hands over the dips and ridges of Eric's abdomen, shuddering at the strength that he found there. His body was cut from a rare diamond, but it was so much more valuable to Zack.

He probed one nipple with his tongue, swirling around it before sucking it into his mouth. It pebbled instantly, and Eric groaned and bucked as Zack scraped his teeth over the bud. He moved his hand to the other nub, pinching it hard, just to hear Eric gasp. He was so responsive, so sensitive, and yet he could take more than most men. By this point, most men would be begging Zack to let them come, but Zack wasn't nearly ready to let that happen.

He shuffled down the bed, looking over his shoulder to check that he wouldn't fall off the edge, before sliding between Eric's spread thighs. He skimmed around Eric's groin, barely touching the fabric of his shorts before moving lower to his thighs. His skin was so smooth, with only fine hairs speckled over the area.

Zack leaned in, placing a lingering kiss on the innermost part of Eric's thigh, where he would be most sensitive. The muscle jumped under his lips and Eric's whole leg twitched.

"This okay?" asked Zack as he placed a second kiss before licking a stripe up the soft skin, tickling the edge of Eric's shorts.

"I-I just want you," said Eric as he threaded his fingers through Zack's hair and started to sit up. Zack stopped him with a gentle hand on his stomach, pushing him back down on the bed.

"Do you trust me?" asked Zack as he looked into Eric's beautiful gold eyes. He waited for Eric's nod before he bit into Eric's thigh hard enough to bruise.

Eric's whole body jerked, and he let out a wail that made Zack second-guess himself. Then he looked up to the tent in Eric's shorts. He was ramrod straight through the fabric, and dripping as he drooled pre-cum.

"Harder," said Eric, his stomach tensing as he pulled himself up, grabbing Zack's hair and pressing him closer. "Fucking bite me."

Zack had never heard Eric swear before. Even when he'd been balls deep, the demon was reserved, each word slow and careful. Zack had assumed it was because Eric was probably older than he could imagine, but maybe it was just because the demon had always held himself back. There was no holding back now.

Despite his aching jaw, Zack bit harder, sinking his teeth into the sensitive flesh. Eric jerked once, flexing his hips into the air, before he fell back, his head thudding into the pillow.

Zack drew back, licking his lips and palming himself to stave off the ache. He was harder than he'd ever been in his life. He dropped his gaze to Eric's lap, and he felt his eyes go wide. The dampness across Eric's groin had spread too much to be the slick pre-cum that he produced. And his hips were still flexing in the same way that he did when he was buried deep within Zack.

Tugging the edge of Eric's shorts, he eased the soaked fabric down to reveal his twitching cock that was still streaming cum from his recent orgasm. There was a lot of it, and still more was flowing as the demon's balls drew up over and over. His knot looked massive, and so much bigger than Zack could ever imagine fitting inside himself. But he had, and it had felt better than anything.

He touched the knot, relishing in the throb and the violent jerk of Eric's hips as he clamped down. He licked along the head, sucking it into his mouth as cum flowed over his tongue and down his throat. It was so peculiar, and different than any cum he'd tasted before, but it was Eric. He was confident that he could identify the demon's spunk blindfolded in a bukkake fest.

Zack gentled Eric through his orgasm, licking and sucking until he couldn't swallow any more, then smeared the rest down Eric's shaft and into the bedding. It was a huge mess, but so worth it to watch Eric's face go from amazed to awed.

When his knot finally started to go down, Zack let go, his hand tingling from holding it for so long. He surged up to Eric's lips, plunging his tongue deep into his mouth to share his taste. Eric sucked him in, as if he were trying to find every last drop in Zack's mouth. He dropped his hands to Zack's ass, squeezing and spreading him wide.

"What's your recovery time like?" asked Zack as he nibbled on Eric's lower lip, soothing the bruise with his tongue.

"I don't know," said Eric as he shifted on the bed, moving them away from the drying wet spot. "Before you, I didn't usually breed out of season, to be honest. And I don't have any recovery time in the spring."

No recovery period. What a blessing and a curse.

"One way to find out," said Zack as he worked his way back down Eric's body, keeping his bites light to try to ease the ache in his jaw. It felt like he'd given head to a dozen men, and the aftertaste in his mouth wasn't helping that image.

He gripped the back of Eric's knees, pushing his legs up and wide until he was completely exposed. He could see the shine of slickness in the low light, a small bead of moisture at the edge of Eric's rim. The furl was clenched tight, and so small that Zack could never imagine being able to sink inside.

Eric's entrance flinched as Zack skimmed his fingertip over it, spreading the slick around. It was enough to ease the slide of his finger, but just. There was no way it would be enough for the kind of fuck he wanted to do. Luckily, he was drooling at the sight before him.

He swiped his finger into his mouth, lathering the joints until they were dripping. When he slid his finger back to Eric, he dipped the tip inside, just enough for the man to feel him. Eric gasped, his body tensing on Zack's finger, making him even more certain that there was no way he was going to fit.

"Are you sure?" Zack asked as he watched Eric flex his stomach muscles, his abdomen rippling. He was almost molten as he stretched around Zack's first joint. If he gripped his cock like this, he might just squeeze it right off.

Eric took a deep breath. "I've never been mounted outside of season either—maybe it's…different?"

Zack nearly wept for Eric. He made it sound like sex was something to be diligently performed once per year. Sex was supposed to be fun, sometimes enough to make you laugh or to make you cry.

"I can try something else," said Zack, pushing Eric's legs wider and lowering himself between them. He licked down Eric's shrunken shaft, revelling in the lingering taste. The demon always seemed to be a least a little bit firm and ready to go at a moment's notice. He twitched now, a spurt of pre-cum dripping from the head and down the naturally slick shaft.

Zack moved lower, to the softness where Eric's knot formed, then to his loose sac. He sucked one side into his mouth, then the other, teasing the sensitive skin. He licked down the seam until he reached the tight entrance that still held his fingertip captive.

It tasted of Eric, only sweeter than his usual smoky flavour. Zack's mouth watered as he swirled around the furled edges, easing his finger out before replacing it with his tongue. The man was sweet like purple clover in spring, and Zack wanted more.

Eric groaned, and suddenly he was relaxing around Zack, his tongue sinking in as far as it could go. Zack licked the rim, delving in and out before sucking along the surface, leaving a bruise along Eric's perineum. Eric keened as Zack accidentally scraped his teeth over his skin.

When Zack slid his finger in this time, he sank to his last knuckle with hardly any effort at all. He curled his finger, searching for the spot that he knew would drive Eric wild. When he heard Eric's low growl, he knew he'd found it.

He worked a second finger in, then a third, plunging into the heat over and over and skimming the man's spot each time. Eric was writhing by the second finger and keening by the third. His cock was hard again and weeping steadily onto his belly.

"I'm close," said Eric on the edge of a whimper as Zack twisted his hand. Zack licked Eric's rim one last time, leaving it dripping before he shuffled back and lined up his cock to the slick hole.

Eric started to come almost as soon as Zack slid into the molten heat, arching his body and clenching, sucking Zack in even deeper. Zack gripped Eric's shaft, ready to squeeze the man's knot, but it never formed. He was coming, that was for sure, but it was the same way Zack did — with a moderate amount of jizz and an above-average dick.

He held himself steady, letting Eric recover, and spreading his cum over his cock as it started to soften again. He waited until Eric's eyes fluttered open before he let himself fall forwards, bringing their lips together and sinking the rest of the way inside.

He moved slowly, barely pulling out, rocking and grinding inside Eric's hole that gripped him with the perfect heat. Their lips slid together, their breaths mingling as they panted together, their hearts beating in sync.

It wasn't fucking. It was making love. It was saying goodbye in the only way Zack could. He wanted to show Eric everything that he meant to him. He wanted Eric to remember this when they were nothing more than memories to each other.

He came slowly as his orgasm built and tipped, shooting his cum deep inside Eric's tight body. Zack groaned against Eric's lips, slamming deep one last time to empty himself. He wanted to stay like that, in the moment, for the rest of his life.

The demon was hard again, his cock pushing insistently against Zack's belly and smearing pre-cum everywhere. Eric gripped Zack's hips, holding him inside until Zack couldn't stand the heat for another second.

He pulled out, crawling up Eric's body and spitting onto his hand. Zack plunged three slick fingers into himself, prying them wide for a second before he straddled Eric and lined up his throbbing cock.

Between the pre-cum coating the tip, the natural slickness of the shaft and Zack's already loosened and spit-slicked hole, the head popped in with only a slight ache. Zack gasped as Eric gripped his hips, his eyes wide with surprise.

"You didn't think we were going to stop at two, did you?" Zack smiled down at Eric, taking a deep breath as he was split wide. Maybe he should have given a bit more than a cursory three fingers. Eric was huge, and even though his knot had stretched Zack wide the night before, it was still a lot.

His legs burned from the strain and his cock jerked, oversensitive and soft as the head of Eric's cock glanced over his prostate. He quirked his hips, changing the angle to avoid the spot. He was too sensitive, and there was no way he was coming again any time soon. It still felt amazing, as his body parted as if he were made for Eric, the man's cock throbbing for him.

"Fuck me, Eric," said Zack as he settled to the base where Eric's knot would form. "Knot me, please." He wanted to feel that swelling flesh as it tugged at his rim and stretched him so wide that he thought he might burst. He wanted to be locked together, so there was no chance that he could leave. He wanted to fall asleep with Eric still inside him, throbbing and spilling himself deep. He wanted to wake up in the morning and feel the stretch where they'd been joined — and the sticky mess between his cheeks.

"Turn around," said Eric, flexing his hands on Zack's ass and forcing him down an extra inch. "I want you to ride me — but turn around."

Zack glanced behind him to Eric's feet. They were big, probably a size eleven or so, with somewhat trimmed toenails and rough cuticles that were in need of a pedicure. They didn't stink at all, but Zack wasn't sure if he wanted to watch them while he was fucking himself on Eric's cock.

"Okay?" said Zack, easing Eric out and scrambling to turn around. He straddled Eric's hips again, gripping his thighs as he lowered himself slowly back down. The angle was slightly different, putting a little bit more pressure on his prostate, until he hunched down, reaching for Eric's knees. It really wasn't the view he wanted.

"Trust me, Zack—just for tonight." Eric grasped Zack's hips, tugging him close at the same time he moved, sitting up and pulling them back to the wall. There was no headboard holding the stark mattress and box spring, so the demon's back must've been pressing directly into the rough wood wall. He didn't seem to mind, though, as he pulled Zack along in his lap.

Eric was all around him. His breath floated over his neck, dancing over the bites that blazed against his skin. His legs were slightly bent, trapping Zack against his groin and back, and leaving him nowhere to go except for down on the cock inside him. They stuck together with their mingling fluids and sweat, panting into the cabin's chilled air.

Then Eric started to move. He rolled and dipped his hips, pushing himself into Zack, but never really withdrawing. Eric gripped him hard, painting fresh bruises along Zack's hips and eclipsing the old ones. His cock, so hard and unyielding, pressed against every spot inside Zack in a way that he'd never imagined.

Cum dribbled from Zack's spent cock as he shuddered through an orgasm that was unlike anything he'd felt before. If beasts could make love, this was exactly how they would do it.

Zack felt Eric's knot strain against his rim, trying to find its way inside, but already growing too big for Zack's body. Eric flexed, forcing himself that much deeper and slipping all the way in with a loud groan.

His knot settled and swelled, locking him into place and stripping every nerve bare in Zack's body. It was so much—too much—as the first jet of cum splashed inside him, filling him deep.

Eric shifted until they were lying on their sides, with his chest to Zack's back and his knot hardly tugging at Zack's rim at all. It felt good, like a butt plug that would keep him ready for his lover.

Not that Zack had much experience with butt plugs… He had bought one when he'd struck out on his own, putting it in the side drawer of his run-down apartment that he'd stayed in for only a few weeks. The plug had been an unfortunate pink and managed to slide out every time he moved in the slightest. But there was no way Eric was popping out anytime soon.

With his balls empty, his cock aching from overstimulation and his body more stretched than ever before, his darkness buzzed under his skin like a threat to everything he loved.

For the first time in his life, he felt complete.

Chapter Twenty

He didn't try to sneak away in the cover of darkness or as the sun first rose over the tips of the snow-dipped trees. He waited until the sun was shining broadly into the cabin, dancing across Eric's skin as they lay together in bed.

The fire had long-since died, leaving the scent of stale ash in the air and a thick chill along the floor. The blanket was pulled up to Zack's shoulders, and he was cradled into Eric's side with his hand splayed across his chiselled stomach.

Zack had awoken clean. Eric had dutifully brushed a cold cloth over his body, scrubbing the blankets the best he could before they had wrapped around each other and fallen asleep. He hadn't been awake for long before he'd felt Eric nudge against him, his cock hard, ready and dripping. He had tilted his hips back the barest inch, and Eric had sunk inside, so slick and hot already. The stretch had hurt, his body barely recovered from the night before, but he'd treasured every moment of ache.

His body throbbed as he laid his head on Eric's chest that was still heaving after just pulling out. He had refused to knot Zack a third time, clamping his hand over his knot and gritting his teeth instead. Zack's cock was utterly spent and practically ready to shoot dust if he tried to come again.

"Breakfast?" asked Eric as he slid his fingers into Zack's hair, tugging the sweaty strands.

Zack shook his head, tipping his face into Eric's chest in an attempt to hide. His stomach was roiling and clenching in the most terrible way, and he knew that if he ate anything, he would just throw it right back up onto the floor. Breakfast meant getting out of the bed…for the last time.

Eric made the decision for him, sitting up so Zack slid sideways off his chest. "You should have breakfast. It's not good for you to go without," said Eric as he stepped out of bed and strode to the bathroom area, dipping the well-used washcloth into a bucket of freezing water.

"I can't eat it. I feel too sick," said Zack, curling tighter as his gut gave another pang with the loss of Eric's body heat. The man was literally a furnace, and Zack was cold on the best of days.

"You'll feel better once you've gone," said Eric as he looked away, the cloth gripped tight in his palm. "Once you get away from here, your curse will fade, and you'll feel so much better."

"I…" Zack rolled over and glared at the ceiling. The spider web was still there, dusty and soft with clinging soot. A week ago, he would've been terrified to wake up with a spider so close to his face, and he would've found a chair and a fly swatter to take care of it, no matter what time of day it was.

Then again, a week ago he'd never taken a shower out of anything but a shower head, and he hadn't been able to go more than a day without finding a place to hook up to Wi-Fi.

But now, he'd had a taste of the simple life, and he had a hard time picturing what it would be like to go back. He could stay with hook-ups again, or in a hotel room if no one was biting. He had the money. His trust fund made sure of that. He had enough money to keep running for the rest of his life.

He only had one place to run from now. At least, as long as the cops believed in his innocence.

"I'll start pushing your car, then," said Eric, without looking back. He tossed on a sweater that would be much too thin for anyone who wasn't a demon, and shorts that belonged on the beach. He didn't even pause to put on shoes, before he pushed his way out of the door, letting it slam behind him.

Zack looked around the cabin after he'd dressed much warmer than Eric. He had the same feeling that he had every time he left a hotel room. There was always some article of clothing that he left behind — a sock under the bed, his watch on the bedstand or a bonus condom somewhere in the sheets.

He wasn't leaving anything physical behind this time, except a few ruined pieces of clothing and some cum-stained sheets, but he was leaving everything else.

Cold air slammed into his face as he stepped outside. The wind had picked up so that, even with the blinding sun, it still felt like he might freeze instantly. His nostrils crinkled and his eyelashes tugged at his lids where frozen tears had glued them together. He was lucky that Eric had found an old pair of soft leather gloves that would keep his fingers from going rigid, but he was still in his running shoes. They were stiff from getting soaked and dried so many times within a few days, but at least he had socks this time.

He'd tried to refuse the clothing, since Eric had hardly anything to begin with, but the demon had ignored him.

The drift on the porch came halfway up Zack's shins, snow already creeping down into his shoes. His first stop after the cop-shop was definitely going to be for some winter boots. He'd never thought that frost bite was an actual thing that people could get now, but the last few days had changed a lot about him.

Eric was standing by the car, the lower half of his body melded with a drift that creeped over the vehicle as the wind whipped through the snow that had fallen over the last few days. Yesterday, he'd been able to see both bumpers, but now they were lost beneath the shifting white mass.

"Once I get it to the road, I'll hang back so you can see if it starts," Eric shouted over the wind as he swept the snow away from the driver's side, popping the door and fiddling with something inside before he leaned back and slammed it shut again.

Even knowing how strong Eric was, Zack still expected him to get some sort of winch or something. He'd seen manly men in the past who had tried to impress him, pulling a muscle opening a pickle jar. He'd also seen a skinny twink take out a six-foot stud with one hit. Now that he thought about it, maybe the twink had been part demon.

Eric circled around to the hood, swiping away a few handfuls of snow so he could put his hands directly on the rusted metal. Then he pushed. The car creaked before starting to roll. The snow parted as if it were extra-light whipped cream and not something that gave old men heart attacks.

He pushed it like it was a dinky car and there was nothing in the way—like he was some kind of Superman that hadn't heard of Kryptonite.

A peek of skin shone through the gap between his sweater and shorts, showing a line of solid muscle that had gone from soft to hard in an instant.

Zack's mouth watered at the sight. There was so much potential with someone that strong, sexual or otherwise…but mostly sexual. Eric had been holding back the entire time, even though he had declared himself to be evil.

A tyre caught on a rut of snow, twisting to the side and sending the car deeper in the wrong direction. Eric paused, ducking inside the car again and straightening the wheel. As soon as he began to push again, it swung left immediately. *Maybe it's another sign?*

"This was a lot easier on the way back here," said Eric as he paused, taking a step back as his chest heaved from the exertion. Sweat glistened on his tanned skin. He looped around the car to the trunk, fiddling with the latch until it popped open. He reached inside, gripping along the frame before he started to pull. His bare feet slipped over the snow, but the car started to move, regardless.

Once the car cleared the rut, it moved as if it were powering itself at low speed over a paved path. Eric's chest heaved and he grunted with each pull, but he never stopped, even as he disappeared down the tiny lane.

Zack strode after him, hefting his bag higher onto his shoulder and taking one last glance back at the cabin. The smoke from the chimney had ceased for the first time since he'd been there, but the rest of it looked like a post card. All he would need is a cardinal perched on the snow-covered roof and he could send it off to Hallmark for a Christmas card.

He hustled along as the forest closed in around him, treading lightly on the grooves from the car's tyres. He thought he would have caught up quickly, but Eric was moving faster than he'd expected. Snow sloshed in his shoes as he ran to catch up, the cold seeping into his lungs and choking him. By the time he caught up, he was out of breath, and the trees were starting to thin.

The first walk to the cabin had seemed to take forever, and his attempted escape route at night had felt like he had walked for hours. In reality, the road was only a few kilometres away — enough that it cut off all sounds of the outside world, but not enough to really be far away from civilization.

Eric was waiting for him with the car perched on the gravel shoulder, the windows already cleared and the chunks of ice gone from the tyres. Eric didn't look up as he approached, but kept his hand pressed to the hood of the car, a print of melted snow dripping down to the road.

He was so beautiful in the light, with the red and gold hues of his long hair glimmering in the sun, and his gold eyes downcast. Zack could see the muscle in his jaw strain as he twitched, grinding his teeth. He clenched his hand into a fist, tapping the hood once before backing away.

"I wanted to thank —"

"Goodbye," said Eric, cutting Zack off with his eyes still downcast. Zack had expected a kiss or at least a fucking hug, but Eric just walked by him, leaving a wide berth as if he were afraid to come close.

Chapter Twenty-One

Zack gripped the freezing steering wheel, feeling the frigid material even through the layered gloves. The car had started with one turn, putting his battery theory to shame. The useless vents blew lukewarm air against the frosted windows until the thin sheet of ice melted away to nothing. The road ahead was clear, with chunks of salt and sand speckling the centre. There wasn't any reason for him not to pull away from the shoulder and not a single other car around that would try to cut him off.

He looked left and right, rubbing his hands together as his darkness slipped away. He'd always imagined it as a cold being in itself, but without it, he felt almost empty, like the frozen wasteland of the Antarctic with only the memory of life buried beneath the snow. Eric was gone, and Zack's curse along with him. He was free.

The last wisp of it fluttered away.

He pulled out onto the road without a turn signal, not even sure which way he was going until he almost ran down into the opposite ditch. He turned back the way he'd come, and towards a life that he'd left in ruins. He could clear things up, mourn for his ex and see his family again for the first time in years. Something fluttered in his belly but wasn't sure if it was hope or terror that he might see his mother again...and his brother. He couldn't even remember how old his brother was now. He might even have kids, for all he knew.

The tyres groaned along the pavement, the car's bearings rusted and worse for wear with its recent snow adventure. He would need a new car for his new life, and he would have to get a job so he could stop dipping into his trust fund at every emergency. He felt guilty about using money that he hadn't earned and really didn't deserve.

How could he deserve it, if he left the only man he had ever loved?

The knot in his stomach grew tighter, and he was glad that he hadn't eaten. He raised his hand to scratch a sudden itch at the back of his neck, accidentally scraping against the scar there. It felt different already, almost numb compared to what it had felt like under Eric's touch. He wondered if the scar itself would fade, too, or if it was just the feeling that would.

"Oh, fuck this," said Zack, slamming on the brakes. They creaked, and the car slowly rumbled as the brakes finally caught, slowing his momentum. They would get him killed in an accident one day, especially if the traction control failed.

He turned the wheel as far as it would go, slamming the gas down and releasing the clutch in one breath. The U-turn was nearly out of control, his hands shaking in time with his pounding heart.

The bald rubber caught at last, twisting the car until he was facing back the way he had come. Snow-covered trees rushed by as he searched the banks for any sign of disturbance. He hadn't driven that far, but the trees all looked identical.

An oncoming car laid on their horn, sending him back into the right lane before they could collide. His chest heaved, filling the car with fog and steaming up the front window as the heater gave one final splutter. He scraped his fingernails against the glass, desperate to clear the ice.

There!

He turned onto the shoulder, landing just down from where the ruts were. He looked around through the frosted glass, searching through the trees but finding nothing. His skin was quiet, with no distant prickling that he had spent his life running from. Eric was gone.

Where the fuck is Eric?

There was no way that Zack was leaving. And Eric had said it himself. If Zack ever came back, he would never let him go again. Zack was counting on it.

He slammed the horn with the heel of his hand, holding it until the trees seemed to vibrate with sound. A blue jay fluttered on a branch, sending an avalanche to the earth as it took flight with a startled *caw* that was muffled by the horn.

Zack drew his hand back as an itch pinched the tips of his fingers, curling up his wrist and wrapping around it, before taking hold and pulling him deep. His heart pounded and he could barely breathe as it fluttered into his chest, stealing his breath and stifling his thoughts. It was terrifying and deadly—but so beautiful.

Eric is coming.

Want to see more from this author?
Here's a taster for you to enjoy!

Greedy Boy
M.C. Roth

Coming June 2022

Excerpt

The building probably had more light switches than any other in the city, but with night pushing against its windows, it was nearly pitch black except for the tiny bleak emergency lights spotted along the stark walls. Within the compartmentalized offices, a few computer screens buzzed, with their colorful screensavers bouncing along with dizzying monotony.

Simon *could* switch the lights on as he crept through the building, but then someone might look up from the street below and wonder what was going on.

The office building emptied at six o'clock sharp every day. One by one the light switches were flicked off, so the entire building went dark as people filed out at the end of their shift. The neighboring condos were bound to contain a few curious souls who would call the cops at the first sign of something out of the ordinary.

Which was something he didn't wanted to risk when he wasn't supposed to be in the office in the first place.

There were only a few company rules that he'd discovered since he'd started working in the grand building a few years before. The strictest of them all was that he was never allowed to work late. His boss had called it a perk. He probably hadn't thought to warn Simon that the deserted halls looked like the inside of a haunted house after dark.

Not that I haven't broken enough rules today.

The biggest rule *should* have been that he wasn't allowed to kiss his boss. It should have been printed in giant gold letters at the top of his orientation papers, which he'd signed for human resources on day one. There had been the salary information, the confidentiality agreement and the listed restrictions to keep employees from stealing clients and going rogue.

There had been nothing about kissing.

Maybe he should have tried harder to pay attention to the sexual harassment video they'd made him watch that had been thirty years out of date? The boredom had been so complete that he had almost passed out in the tiny plastic folding chair.

The kiss hadn't been his fault!

* * * *

Six hours earlier

Simon let out a tired sigh as he organized a few things on his desk and filed a frustrating contract under 'G' as he got ready to wrap up the rest of his paperwork. Six o'clock was looming close, only an hour away according to the digital clock at the corner of his computer screen. Sixty minutes before he would head out of the door and into the swarming hive that was public transportation.

He reached for his bag, the fabric slipping against his fingertips, when he heard a sound coming from his boss's office—his very quiet and very professional boss, who hadn't even shouted when he'd stubbed his toe on his desk two days before.

He peeked in the office door, knowing that he didn't have to knock. Rich, dark wood filled the space that was decorated with expensive art and a bookshelf with a few first edition novels.

Rubric Mayvel, one of the richest and most desired men in the country, was facing his office window that overlooked the bustling city below. His shoulders were heaving, the rumpled fabric of his shirt stretched tight. The shattered remains of a shot glass lay among the carpet fibers, the bitterness of expensive bourbon in the air.

Drops of alcohol flowed down the window, and the tiny shards of glass stranded in the carpet glinted in the afternoon light. Mr. Mayvel didn't seem to notice the state of the window or the glass, his gaze drawn to the rushing traffic of the city below.

Simon didn't think twice before he rushed in, grabbing the small broom and dustpan that always hung conveniently by the door. Sweeping up a little bit of glass was nothing worse than having Mr. Mayvel's morning coffee ready for him when he strolled into the office five minutes early, his suit pressed and perfectly fitted on his tall, sleek body.

Simon copied, signed, faxed, emailed and did every other imaginable thing to the paperwork that went through his boss's office, so a little bit of glass on the floor wasn't beneath him. He was there to help, after all.

It was the same reason that Simon shielded his boss from solicitors, usually feeling terrible about hanging up on someone who was just trying to make a living. He even acted as a tiny guard outside Mr. Mayvel's office, mostly keeping secretaries or other interlopers away and distracting them by asking for details on the latest gossip.

Simon had a face that people liked to tell their secrets to, and he knew exactly who was screwing who in the office because of it—all seventy floors included. Not that he would ever tell anyone about what he learned or look at any of his colleagues differently. So what if Niamo had her boyfriend tie her up? That actually sounded kind of hot.

Kneeling on the office floor, he scraped the glass into the trash bin, leaving the stained window for the cleaners, knowing he would just make the smearing worse. He poured a glass of ice water, setting it on the desk before he prepared to retreat.

Mr. Mayvel hadn't looked away from the window when Simon had entered the room or when he'd bent over to pick a few stray shards out of the carpet, but that was nothing new.

Simon did his duties with as little inconvenience to Mr. Mayvel as possible, not to mention that Simon had the approximate sex appeal of flat ginger ale, while Mr. Mayvel put models to shame.

But when he started to back out of the room, he looked up to see Mr. Mayvel staring at him, as if he had lost his way while gazing out of the windowpane. His shoulders were slumped, and his suit was crumpled in a way that Simon had never seen before. His hair was limp from him running his hands through it over and over, and there were dark smudges under his eyes that Simon hadn't noticed earlier in the day.

"Are you okay?" Simon asked as he folded his hands behind his back to keep from fiddling. Mr. Mayvel always commented if Simon clicked his pen too many times or tapped his fingers on his desk while he was thinking.

The sky flamed golden in the afternoon light, shimmering against Mr. Mayvel's honey-colored hair and turning it almost bronze. The sight pulled at Simon, begging him to step closer.

Mr. Mayvel caught his gaze, dragging his tongue over his lower lip that looked swollen, as if he'd been chewing on it in distress. Simon wanted to speak up and ask Mr. Mayvel what he could do to help, but he was mesmerized by the sight. He would do anything the man needed, if only to take the broken look off his face.

Simon didn't realize that his *anything* included moving closer and cupping his boss's cheek in his palm. Mr. Mayvel leaned into the touch, his long lashes dancing over his cheeks as he closed his eyes. He was so beautiful but so lost.

Lifting up to the tips of his toes, Simon brought their lips together. He'd never imagined kissing Mr. Mayvel before, because he had kept the man squarely in the 'off-limits' corner of his mind.

Mr. Mayvel's lips were soft, yet firm, the lower one a bit swollen and warmer against his own. At the first touch, heat seared between them, building so quickly that Simon's reservations quickly spiraled beyond his control. Mr. Mayvel let out the smallest gasp, and Simon pushed into his mouth with a groan, tasting bourbon along with the faintest hint of cigarettes.

He wasn't sure how long they kissed as he took complete control, even with his shorter stature. Mr. Mayvel showed no signs of resisting or fighting for dominance, melting against Simon like smooth chocolate. It was the sweetest kiss Simon could remember from the last year, if not longer, and it was with his boss.

Simon finally pulled back with dawning horror, ripping his hands away from where he had accidentally buried them in Mr. Mayvel's hair. Mr. Mayvel's lips were kiss-swollen and red, glistening as the sun peeked through the window. His eyes were half-lidded, with a blush across his cheeks that hid the darkness of the smudges under his eyes.

"I-I'm…"

It was the only thing that Simon managed to say before he turned and fled, pushing his way out of the office. His lips tingled, and he touched them as he rounded the corner, remembering the way Mr. Mayvel's mouth had felt against his.

How was he going to find a new job? His stomach sank as his heart pounded.

When he reached the elevator, he ran through the doors, pressing his back against the wall as he waited for the gates to close. His breaths came in short gasps, his vision starting to blot as he approached hyperventilation. His stomach twisted into so many knots he wasn't sure if he would ever be able to eat again.

"You okay, Simon?" Troy asked with a raised brow as he took a sip from his coffee mug. Simon hadn't noticed his coworker standing in the elevator when he had thrown himself inside.

A flush bloomed on his face. "S-sorry! I just f-forgot I had an appointment t-today and had to leave a f-few minutes early, so I'm running," Simon stammered, flushing hotter as the lie stuck on his tongue. He couldn't exactly tell Troy the truth, but the lie lay deep in the pit of his stomach, making him even heavier.

"Hmm-m," Troy said, tapping his finger to his lip before he pressed the back of his hand to Simon's forehead. "You might be getting sick, Simon. I've never heard of you forgetting anything, least of all an appointment. You are a bit flushed. Make sure you get straight to bed after." He pulled away, hitting the button for the parking garage and the main floor.

Troy had his own car there—a monstrosity of a Jeep that belonged to one or both of his boyfriends—but he knew that Simon took the bus home.

"Thanks, Troy." Simon melted against the back of the elevator as he tried to slow his breathing.

About the Author

M.C. Roth lives in Canada and loves every season, even the dreaded Canadian winter. She graduated with honours from the Associate Diploma Program in Veterinary Technology at the University of Guelph before choosing a different career path.

Between caring for her young son, spending time with her husband, and feeding treats to her menagerie of animals, she still spends every spare second devoted to her passion for writing.

She loves growing peppers that are hot enough to make grown men cry, but she doesn't like spicy food herself. Her favourite thing, other than writing of course, is to find a quiet place in the wilderness and listen to the birds while dreaming about the gorgeous men in her head.

M.C. Roth loves to hear from readers. You can find her contact information, website details and author profile page at https://www.pride-publishing.com

PUBLISHING

Sign up for our newsletter and find out about all our
romance book releases, eBook sales and promotions,
sneak peeks and FREE romance books!